HOLIDAY SPIRIT FOR HIRE

Otherworld Realms: Book Two

Isabelle Saint-Michael

Otherworld Romance, llc

Copyright © 2014 by Isabelle Saint-Michael.
All rights reserved.

Published by Otherworld Romance, llc
www.otherworldromance.com
www.elvenlife.com

ISBN 978-0-9908665-2-7

A special thanks to all of my little helpers

And the warmest wishes to all of my readers

Chapter One

I stared out the window as the grey rain beat against the pavement outside. I had moved to Portland three years ago and hadn't seen snow since. Then again, the Monday after Thanksgiving was always depressing. Everyone overspent on Black Friday sales or had to be up entirely too early to put in-laws on a plane to go home. Christmas in Portland was nothing like Christmas in Connecticut. Starting with the absence of white fluffy snow.

"Grace!" I jumped as my name was snapped loudly, then winced as I slammed my knee into the desk while spinning around to face my boss. Bob towered over me even more than usual today. Everything about the man was big. He was six foot six and probably as big around. His voice was monstrous and echoed through the office even when he was *trying* to whisper.

"Yes, Bob, what can I do for you, sir?" I asked in my most upbeat voice.

"I paged you three times and you didn't answer. I was beginning to wonder if you came to work today."

He had said hello to me when I entered the office an hour late this morning. He knew darn well I had come to work.

"I'm sorry, I guess I'm just recovering from the weekend," I told him.

"Ah, well, we are having an office-wide meeting at three. Can you make sure everyone is in the conference room at that time?" he asked, his voice much softer.

I had heard a dirty rumor around the water cooler that we weren't getting holiday bonuses this year because of rough second and third quarters. I respected Bob for letting us know early so hopefully people could make arrangements to budget the holidays without it. I put together a mass email that we had a meeting at three and shot it out to all twenty members of staff.

I absentmindedly poked through the reports looking for a missing piece of information I needed to complete the requested forms for a client. Every few clicks of a mouse I found myself turning to look at the rain. At ten till three my computer reminded me I had a meeting to attend. I grabbed a notepad and pen and headed down the hall.

We all crammed into our tiny conference room meant for six people or less. At three o'clock Bob walked in with a stack of envelopes in his hand. A murmur went through the group as we eyed the stack. Something was off. Bob never gave bonuses until the week of Christmas and when he did, he was always happy. Last year he even dressed up as Santa and encouraged the office ladies to sit on his lap. No, Bob didn't look like a jolly Santa prepared to hand out holiday cheer.

Then it hit me. Before he even started talking my stomach was already in knots. "As all of you know, it's been a really rough year here. Last week I was forced to sell the company to a buyer based in upstate New York. I have here your pay for the time you've worked through the end of this week. I'm really sorry, but I have to let you all go." Big, loud Bob looked miserable. "Also, there are members of the new company here to help you clear out your belongings. I know none of you would do it, but please don't take any of the company assets."

I waited in line with everyone to get my check. When everyone but me had received theirs Bob looked up at me. "Can you close the door?" he asked.

Obeying, I shut the door and turned to face him. "Gracie, I know I moved you out here from the East Coast and it hasn't been easy for you. Everyone else in the office is a native Pacific North-Westerner. I spoke with the new owner and let him know that you are from out that way. He said if you contact him after the first of the year he will see if he can find a place for you in the company out East." He sighed heavily. "I know it's not much, but I have included an airline voucher from cashing in some of my miles. It should be enough to get you home to see your family this Christmas, and maybe you can get a lead on something job-wise closer to home."

I was shocked. It was a sweet and thoughtful favor. "Thank you, I know you've had this business for a long time. What are you going to do now?"

"Well, the wife and I talked it over. We have a nice nest egg and did alright in the buyout. I think I'm going to retire early and spend time with my girls and the grandkids." He stood up and offered me his arms. I nodded and gave him a hug, barely reaching his chest. "And if you need a recommendation or anything you just have them call or email me, alright?"

"Thanks, Bob. Tell Linda and the girls Merry Christmas for me." I turned and left the conference room. When I got back to my desk I found a short man in a black suit carefully putting my personal belongings into a file box.

"Is this lamp your personal lamp or does it belong to the office?" he asked. His voice was surprisingly deep for his size.

"It's mine," I said. I watched him with interest as he wrapped bubble wrap around it and placed it in the box.

"Please come take one last look through the desk for any other personal belongings I might have missed. Then I can escort you to your car, Ms. MacGregor." Hearing him call me by my last name surprised me. Everyone called me Grace or Gracie.

I poked through the desk, finding a photo of me in Scotland visiting my cousins and a package of pop tarts. With a shrug I put them both in the box and pulled on my coat. He picked up the box and walked with me out the door and to my car. I unlocked the trunk and he was nice enough to load the box for me. "Thank you...?" I looked for a nametag but couldn't find one.

"Darren, my name is Darren. You're welcome Ms. MacGregor. I'm sorry this had to happen so close to the holidays." His voice was surprisingly warm for having such a deep rumble.

"Not your fault. Thanks for the help with the box. Happy Holidays, Darren." With a click of the lock I opened the door and got in. He stood in the rain and watched me leave. He probably had to account for each employee leaving the premises.

I flipped on the radio but every station was playing carols. Finally giving up, I just left it tuned to some jazz version of Jingle bells and focused on the drive home. Even though it rains in Portland three hundred and sixty two days out of the year, every driver was acting like it was the first time they had driven in the rain. Ten miles felt like an eternity when I finally pulled into the parking lot of my apartment complex.

I looked around at the drab grey buildings that matched the weather and stomped through the puddles to my front door. Grey gloom was a very normal look for this time of year, but it was definitely one if those depressing kind of days that made it feel like the storm cloud was on a personal mission to haunt you. I grabbed the paper off the covered stoop, unlocked the door and stepped inside. The first thing I saw was my pile of Christmas decorations that I now had no interest in putting up.

I changed into pajamas, flipped the TV on and grabbed my take-out containers from the prior night's dinner. I needed to call my folks. Dad would know what to do. He'd been through this at least three dozen times over the centuries. Since my father and mother bonded ninety-one years ago they've had to move a lot so people wouldn't notice they never really aged. I always wondered why they didn't go back to Scotland to be closer to his family where they wouldn't need to move so often.

Picking up the phone I hit pound four and listened as the phone rang. "Hello? Gracie? You're calling early. Was everyone recovering from the weekend?" Mom's voice always sounded cheerful.

"No, not exactly. The company was sold last week. We all came in today to find out we were being laid off. Is Dad there?" My mom was silent on the other end of the phone.

There was a rustling noise followed by the sounds of shuffling paper. "Dad's not here right now but Mom went to get her credit card. What's going on?" My brother Michael's voice was mellow and relaxed.

"I was laid off. Why is Mom getting her credit card?" I had a sneaky feeling that if I didn't put my foot down my mother would be here before the week was over.

"She's booking a flight I think." He seemed amused by the whole ordeal.

"Stop her, Michael!" I heard soft arguing in the background then a load crack followed by Michael howling. Mom must have the wooden spoon on hand.

There was more rustling on the phone. "Dear, your brother is under the impression you don't want me to come." I rolled my eyes, realizing this was going to be a delicate operation.

"Mom, don't worry about it. I have enough airline miles to come see you for Christmas this year. I'm going to have a good cry, eat some cookie dough, then start looking for a new job first thing in the morning. Don't worry about me. Besides, I'm sure you have plenty to do for the holidays already." I heard her sniffle a bit.

She cleared her throat. "Well if that's how you feel... I understand. I guess you don't need me anymore." I cringed. Her tone told me everything I needed to know. She was upset. If she was upset, Dad would be upset when he found out. Ugh.

"Mom, I promise to call in the morning. I love you." She started to say something else but instead opted to return the normal exchange and part ways. I powered the phone off and sat it on the coffee table.

The TV flashed back to the Holiday special about a little girl finding a new husband for her mother for Christmas. I almost gagged at the sickeningly sweet story. Nothing like this happened. People don't just fall in love and get married all between Thanksgiving and Christmas. I flipped the TV off and put the leftovers back in the fridge before grabbing a tube of cookie dough and gnawing off a bite. I considered the tube carefully, then put it away and decided bed and resume work was a more productive option.

I settled into bed with my favorite boyfriend, my laptop. Before long I had updated my resume, applied for a half dozen jobs, checked flights home, and Facebooked with all of my friends to see if anyone had any leads. I was about to shut down when the pop from my email caught my attention.

I closed the other tabs and stared at my inbox. It was from the OAC. The Otherworld Alignment Council was a group of magical beings, things that go bump in the night, and people that made sure that there were universal laws and regulations used across all the realms. They made sure there was a common language, rules about magic, and laws that kept peace between the different races. Why they were emailing me I didn't know.

To: Grace MacGregor

From: OAC

Subject: The North Pole Needs You

Dear Ms. MacGregor,

It has been brought to the attention of the OAC that you are no longer employed during this busy time of the year. Every Holiday season we rely on the help we get from the Otherworld community to make the season bright. Your talents could be used now through the end of the year helping deliver joyful winter holidays across all the realms.

Please see the attached application. Applicants will be considered for a paid position. Please send a resume, two letters of recommendation and magical aptitude test scores to the email listed below. If chosen we will need you to report immediately for work.

Thank you and Happy Holidays,

Otherworld Alignment Council

I looked at the email again and shrugged. "Why not?" I asked myself. I attached my resume, two recommendation letters and a quick note explaining my father was a Scottish Werewolf Clansman and that I was half human. I figured my lack of magical abilities would keep me out of the fray. My father told me to always answer the OAC right when they contacted you because they made the IRS look patient.

With a giggle to myself I closed the windows on my laptop and shut it down. Snuggling deep into my pillows I closed my eyes, giggling about what use I could possibly be to the Great Holiday Front up North. Strangely enough I fell asleep with thoughts of sugar plums dancing in my head

Chapter Two

I awoke the next morning to the sounds of clinking, clicking and power tools. I opened my eyes involuntarily when a particularly loud noise sounded right over my head. It was then I noticed my bedroom was swarming with Gnomes and they seemed too busy to care I was sleeping.

"Excuse me!" I yelled. "Why are you in my bedroom?"

A few of them stopped, exchanged looks with shrugs, and returned to work. I wasn't answered until a man with a heavy red braid down his back appeared.

"You are in their workshop, and it's about time you got up." I climbed out of bed angrily, prepared to demand that they leave. "Nice pajamas," he said with a grin as he looked me over. "If you follow me we will get you assigned duties, uniforms and the rest of your paperwork filled out."

I looked around what should have been my room. I was on a toy factory floor. Only it looked like FAO

Schwarz met Ikea. Bright colors with industrial-grade shelves mixed with the old world charm of hand-carved wooden trim. All around me Gnomes were hustling to complete toys. I looked in the direction the redheaded man had gone and chased after him, abandoning my bed to the factory.

I ran down the hall, ignoring curious glances from the people I passed. I crashed into him as he stopped in front of a door marked "Fae and Darkling Resources". I started to tumble to the floor but a well-placed arm around my waist spun me around and sat me back on my feet. "Whoa there, I'm sure you're excited to get started, but let's avoid workplace mishaps, shall we?"

I followed him into a small office that housed a single desk. He motioned for me to have a seat. The office was rather bland - white walls with a simple wooden desk. A sleek laptop, a single Christmas card, and a coffee mug reading "Dwarves do it better" were the only personal items in the office. "I'm sorry, where am I and how did I get here?" I asked, staring at the coffee mug.

"You applied to work on the Holiday Front this year. When your hiring was approved you were brought here to begin work immediately. We were

VERY surprised to find you sleeping your first day on the job but it's your first time so we'll let it slide." He smiled warmly. His eyes sparkled like green emeralds set against a velvety background. A single dimple lit up his face.

"We?" I asked, shaking my head to clear it.

"Yes, North Pole Operations." He read my confusion. "You applied last night through the OAC for a position for the Holiday Season. I approved your hire this morning at three AM. You were then brought here." He took a long sip from his coffee cup.

"You hired me at three AM and expected me to be ready?" I crossed my arms over my chest. "What about an interview? What about a job offer?" I really didn't fancy waking up in a toy factory.

"Yeah, I don't have much experience with Halflings. Most of the ones I have had the pleasure of meeting are split magical beings, not half human. I was a little surprised, but you have an excellent referral, went to a top University, and had a solid work history so I figured why not give you a shot." He sat the cup down and typed something into the laptop.

"I'm sorry for staring but I thought Dwarves were shorter, with beards, and dressed like Celts or Vikings?" The words just sort of slipped out.

He chuckled. It was a rich sort of sound that made me think of chocolate truffles and thick sweaters. "I guess if you have only lived in the Human realm all your life, Lord of the Rings would do that to you. I may decide to grow a beard in another few centuries, but it won't be anytime soon. My uncle doesn't even wear a beard anymore and he's the current Santa." He smiled again. "As for short, I'm short when compared to an Elf or even a modern Human but five seven hardly seems abnormally small. Just... well, short," he said with a shrug.

I shook my head trying to take it all in. "I'm sorry, I'm Gracie MacGregor..."

He cut me off. "No, I'm sorry. I'm Justin Kringle." He held out his hand to shake mine. Without hesitation I accepted his but wasn't quite prepared for the heavy shake I got. "Oh, sorry about that. Don't always remember my own strength."

"So I'm at the North Pole, in my pajamas, and you're the nephew of Santa?" I just wanted to make sure I was getting this entire delusion right.

"Yup," he answered, sliding a pile of papers and a pen across the desk. "And if you could just get started filling these out I would really appreciate it."

I looked down at the stack of papers. "What is my job going to be? How much am I going to be paid?"

"Wow, you really are Human aren't you?" He took the stack of paper back and highlighted a job title and salary, then slid it back to me. I tried not to gag when I saw the salary. It was more than double what I was earning a month working for Bob.

"What exactly is a Holiday Spirit?" I inquired hesitantly.

"Well, you will be assigned cases where the joy of the season is needed. Once you have a case it is your responsibility to make sure that optimal Holiday Enjoyment is achieved." He held out the pen.

"I go around making people happy?" It sounded too good to be true. "Like giving bikes to orphans and helping puppies find homes?"

"Something like that," he answered with a slight quirk of his brow that told me I had just oversimplified it.

"What if I don't believe in holiday spirit?" I retorted quickly.

"Then you will really suck at your job and won't be paid. If you read the contract, you have twenty-two days to complete at least ten cases if you expect to be paid." He nodded to the pen.

"I was an executive assistant, I used to put out more than ten fires before lunch every day. How hard can it be?" I took the pen, signing and initialing my way through the pile of papers.

"Excellent, now that the paperwork is all set let's get you a uniform and some magic." I blinked at his words but he led me out of the office. Just down the hall and to the right was a large green metal door. Justin pushed it open, revealing a room where hundreds, if not thousands, of costumes hung on a garment conveyer like one would find at a drycleaners. "Hi there Maggie, I have a new Holiday Spirit in need of a uniform and magic."

A short Gnome dressed all in blue looked at me from her chair. Her cheeks were rosy, her eyes twinkled and her mouth was drawn up in a disapproving sneer. "A Werewolf-Human Halfling? The council must really be scraping the bottom of the bucket these days." I fought down the urge to tell her just exactly who I was.

She looked me over. "Normally they bring me pretty, thin Elves or beautiful, dainty Fairies. I'm not sure I have anything that will fit her." Her tone was flat and barely hid her lack of approval.

I looked down at myself. While I wasn't supermodel thin, I took pretty good care of myself. I had curves for sure, but my waist was narrow and I knew my assets were appealing to the opposite gender. The woman pulled several articles from hangers and bins before tossing them on the counter.

First she held up a long white dress that seemed practically transparent. It had a cape made of the same fabric. I hoped my job was indoors and well heated. Next was a cumbersome hat that looked like it had started life as a wreath that lost a fight with a florist and things didn't get better from there. The final accessory was a pouch that held sparkling dust that looked like the fake glitter-snow malls used to decorate with. "Here you go, missy." She handed me a clipboard. "All articles are to be worn anytime you are out doing field work. Any damages to the items will be taken out of your pay. Please sign the release."

I scribbled a signature on the paper and handed it back.

"Thanks, Maggie, you're a doll. I'll see you tonight at the productivity meeting, right?" Justin made it seem like the North Pole was all business and no fun, but he was so cheerful as he did it. Maggie the Gnome blushed and waved him away. Justin turned to me.

"Now, if you follow me one last time I will show you to the dorms where you will be staying this month, and the office as well. I'm sure you want to get started as soon as possible." His smile was beginning to look a little too energetic to me.

When we arrived at the dorms I stood just inside the doorway while he talked to the manager. Every time someone came in or out a gust of arctic air would hit me. All I was wearing were my pajamas. When Justin finally came back it was to find me turning blue and shaking.

"We have a small problem."

I knew I wasn't going to like the answer. "What sort of problem?"

"We're out of space. Not to worry though, I will take you over to the Dwarven housing and see if I can find a spare room or something for you. There are many of us who live here year-round so the housing over there is a little homier. The down side is there are no shuttles to the office or facilities so you'll need to walk or see if you can arrange rides." He seemed satisfied with his answer.

"How far is it from here?" I was already freezing just from standing in the doorway.

"Not too far, maybe a fifteen or twenty minute jaunt." He opened the door and I was smacked full force with icy air. He held the door open and motioned for me to go ahead.

He said jaunt like it was the distance from the front door to the end of the driveway where one would pick up the morning paper. A distance that when walked at a leisurely pace took less than a minute to cover. The one mile hike in blistering cold weather was not a jaunt.

My feet were freezing in the slipper socks I wore and I had stopped shaking. In fact I was starting to realize I was really rather sleepy. I was so tired, I noticed my vision was starting to blur a little. I stumbled trying to keep up with Justin. I could hear him talking but couldn't understand a word he was saying.

Finally, he stopped and turned to say something to me. His eyes widened in surprise and he quickly closed the few steps between us. "You're turning blue! I didn't know Humans or Werewolves did that."

I tried to answer but nothing came out but a squeak. His face went from surprised to alarmed in the blink of an eye. He looked around us and seemed upset when he didn't see what he was looking for. In one fluid motion he scooped me up in his arms and began to dash through the snow.

In just a few short moments I was in a large blue chair sitting by a fire as he heaped piles of blankets on me. He dashed out of the room, returning moments later with a basin of warm water. He knelt to peel the socks from my feet and slid the water basin under them. I sucked in air at how hot it felt. "Wow that's hot!" I said trying to pull me feet out of it. He reached up, holding my knees in place.

"Actually it's room temperature at best. You almost have frostbite and probably have hypothermia. What were you thinking coming to the North Pole dressed like that? I thought it was some weird Werewolf thing that let you stay warm."

If I could have moved I would have boxed his ears. He knew I had arrived in my pajamas. He saw me get out of bed.

"Where I'm from we don't kidnap people bed and all to have them start working. If we are going to relocate them we give them at least a few hours to pack and possibly a packing list. I submitted the application and went to bed. What did you expect?" I didn't mean to be rude but I was more than a little frustrated with the situation.

"What I expect is for you to be professional. Did you know you were applying to work with a magical organization?" His tone matched mine.

"Yes," I answered.

"Did the job posting mention the North Pole?" he asked, becoming more irritated.

"Yes," I nodded.

"Then what did you think this was? We service the Yule, Christmas, Winter Festival, Bleak Days and so on season for ALL THE REALMS. Billions if not trillions count on us and our magic to make the season bright. If you weren't interested in the job, why did you apply?" His final words were edged with a harsh tone.

I bit my lip for a moment staring daggers at him. "Look, Grace, my job isn't to be your friend. My job is to make sure things get done. And guess what?" I quirked a brow at him. "From now until Christmas Eve, that's your job too."

I was finally able to wiggle my toes again. When Justin noticed he added actual hot water to the basin. Sighing in frustration he looked up at me before standing. "You stay here. I'm going to find you a place to stay and I'll see if I can track down some clothes you can wear. Hopefully you can wear Dwarven clothes." He stormed out of the room closing the door behind him.

For the first time I looked around the room I was in. It felt more like a cottage. A large log bed sat in the corner covered in pillows, quilts, furs and blankets. A single window ran the full length of the room allowing the snow fluttering in lamplight to dance in the wind. The wall with the fireplace had four wooden bookshelves, each with intricate carvings of holly, snowflakes and northern animals. The shelves held a mixture of books, photos, and other personal mementos. The mantle was covered in the same ornamental carvings as the bookshelves. Above the fireplace were a collection of family photos, many of them with Justin. He had brought me to his personal quarters. I was sure there were rules for that too.

The only other furniture in the dwelling was a rustic wooden table and a matching blue ottoman. The man lived simply. Comfortably, but simply. I looked back at the photos. Many of them showed a smile that was carefree. His lone dimple acted like a beacon pulling the viewer into the joy of the moment.

My thoughts were interrupted when the owner of said dimple came back in the front door stomping his feet and swearing under his breath. His arms were filled with what looked like clothes but the look on his face didn't seem like someone who had returned victorious. I started to stand to come help him with his armload but he snapped at me to stay seated.

"Well, I have good news and bad news. Which would you like first?" He dumped the pile of clothes on his bed.

"Well, let's get the painful part over with first. Always better to just rip off the bandage." I offered a half-hearted smile.

"We don't have any rooms left. All of my sisters are doubled up in their quarters already. As are all my female cousins. I tried to see if we could free up a bed anywhere. I found a cot, and as I am the only person not sharing a room, guess who your new bunkmate is." He smiled sarcastically. "I was very set against sharing my room with a female, especially one I'm not related to or involved with."

I shrugged. "I grew up with brothers. When I visit the family in Scotland we all sort of pile in. Werewolves tend to sleep with their packs and clans. So when I went with my parents I slept in a den with a dozen others. I can handle a cot."

He raised a brow at me. "Besides the whole male-female thing, it's totally inappropriate because I am your superior."

"Do you plan on seducing me?" My blunt question seemed to affect him as if I had slapped him.

He sputtered and mumbled. "Of course not! I am a Dwarven gentleman. I assure you I am honorable."

I giggled without meaning to. I buried my face in my hands trying to quell the need to laugh. When I removed them to speak I was still smiling. Justin stared at my smile in an almost trance-like state.

"If you're not going to seduce me then I doubt there is a reason to be concerned, right?" He just nodded.

"I have nothing to fear from you because you are a gentleman with honorable intentions. Problem solved. Any other bad news?" He shook his head, still silent. "Then what is the good news?"

"Huh?" was all he said.

"I said, what is the good news?" I pursed my lips, still grinning, trying not to giggle.

"Oh, right! Sorry." He looked down; slightly embarrassed by his unresponsiveness. "I was able to get a selection of clothes. You should see if any of these fit."

I started to get up but he rushed over and urged me to sit back down. He then knelt again to check my feet.

"They look like they will be ok. You'll want to keep your feet and head warm here as much as possible." He grabbed a small towel and patted away the worst of the moisture.

I made my way to the bed and dug through the pile of clothes. There were a half dozen pairs of pants and sweaters, a hat, a wool coat, wool socks, a scarf and boots. I tugged off my pajamas and pulled a pair of pants, a sweater and socks on.

When I turned to face Justin again I discovered he was as red as a berry. "What's wrong?"

"You were, umm, well... just now." There was something strangely adorable about him not being able to put together words.

"Naked?" I offered.

"Yeah, that," he said pointing at me. I laughed and waved it away.

"I'm sorry. Werewolf family, sort of destroys any semblance of modesty someone may have. It wasn't until high school that my father or brothers started wearing any clothes around the house. I brought a few friends home to study one day and, well, let's say there were some angry phone calls." I shrugged.

He laughed. "Did you and your brothers get the Were genes?"

"Sort of, I guess all three of us got it to various degrees. If we complete the Darkling rituals we can actually become full Were but I'm not sure that's something any of the three of us want."

I folded the clothes on the bed. "Where should I put these?"

He held out his arms and took the clothes. "Over here," he nodded to an empty wall. "Push on that knot in the wood."

I looked at the wood paneling but did what he said. To my amazement the panel slid open, revealing a closet. While nothing huge, it was certainly bigger than what I had in Portland. He stacked the clothes on a shelf that didn't have much on it.

He slid the door shut. "If you're staying with me let's set some ground rules. Music will only be listened to on headphones from eleven PM to eight AM. I don't like things messy so while it is fine to eat in here make sure all plates make it back to the kitchen before you go to bed. If you put your boots on I will show you where the bathroom, kitchen, dining room and main hall are. Mind you, these are all part of the family house so normally outsiders would eat, sleep, etc. at the dorms, but at night you can stay on this side of the campus during nonworking hours."

I tugged the boots on, happy when they fit well enough, and grabbed the coat as I stepped out the door behind him. Shrugging the coat on I walked across an entryway and through another door. It led into a large kitchen that looked like it belonged in a gingerbread house. Grabbing my wrist, Justin led me through the house, showing me several bathrooms to choose from, many equipped with multiple showers, sinks and toilets. The final room was large with a vaulted ceiling. It looked like a modern log cabin with a massive fireplace, several groupings of large plush chairs, ottomans and sofas. The gem of the room was a sparkling fifteen foot tree covered in every type of ornament imaginable.

"It's beautiful," I said breathlessly.

"Yeah, we're pretty fond of it. You are welcome to anything in the fridge or cupboards that doesn't have a note on it. Feel free to read any books or watch movies if you have down time. Welcome to your home for the next three weeks."

He started to turn to leave. "Oh and don't mention to anyone not in the family that you're staying in the main house. We wouldn't want anyone to get the wrong idea." Before I could respond he was headed out the door back to his quarters.

"Wait, aren't you going to show me the office? What about my bed in the workshop? Who do I need to report to in order to start... spiriting?" I asked in a flurry of questions.

"I'll have your bed sent home for you. I'll take you to the office now if you want to get started right away." He seemed to relax a little at the news I wanted to get started.

As we left the house, he turned towards a small barn. Inside were a half-dozen snowmobiles. "You never saw these," he said, holding a finger up to his mouth.

"Mum's the word." When he climbed on one I was a little hesitant. I remembered riding them as a kid. I also remembered falling off the back of one in college and needing stitches. With a quick, silent prayer I climbed on behind him.

"Hold on tight." I wrapped my arms around him and was surprised when he gave them a tug, pulling them tighter.

With a loud roar we rushed through the afternoon snow back towards the workshop facilities. Before we reached it we turned down a path and parked the snowmobile next to a few others out of sight.

"Ok, let's get you set up and running."

An hour later I was settled into a desk staring at snow tumbling down outside. I smiled. It was exactly what I had all but wished for the day before. I turned my attention to a pile of folders in front of me. My job was to read the files then go and orchestrate things so a holiday miracle took place without causing harm to others. So obviously I couldn't use magic to make a store give a bunch of bikes to orphans if it meant the store wouldn't make enough money to pay the bills.

Work holiday magic and don't be seen. When I asked why I had to wear the flimsy costume if I wasn't to be seen I was given the answer of, "Just in case." Lame!

The first case seemed pretty easy. A soup kitchen in Pittsburgh had to turn people away because they didn't have enough food to feed all those in need. It took me all afternoon but I managed to convince four local restaurants to bring the extra food they would normally need to toss at the end of the day to the soup kitchen. By six I had all the needed paperwork in their hands so they received the charitable tax write-off, and the soup kitchen had enough donations to keep people fed.

"One down, nine more to go." I smiled as I looked at the clock. It was a quarter of eight by the time I wrapped up. I realized just how hungry I was when my stomach protested. I'd skipped lunch and hadn't eaten all day. I gathered up a few files and tucked them into my coat. I planned to start reviewing them tonight before bed. I hoped the kitchen had something warm to eat.

When I trudged back to the house I stepped into the kitchen rather than Justin's quarters. I could hear many people in the dining room laughing and conversing. I considered for a moment going in to say hello, but instead made a plate and took it along with a hot cup of coffee back to the room.

I pulled the small table over to the fire and the large blue chair, careful not to spill any of the food that I had set on it. I went to the closet to see if there was something more sleep-worthy in the things he had brought me earlier. When I didn't find anything I pulled out an old flannel shirt that looked like it didn't see much use anymore. I tossed it over the back of the chair, then sat and ate.

When I finished I returned the plate to the kitchen, and went to find a shower. The bathrooms were deserted. It sounded like everyone was still in the dining room or great room. After my shower I pulled on the flannel, folded my clothes from the day and darted barefoot down the hall, through the kitchen and back across the snowy entranceway. I had realized walking around in nothing but a flannel may be frowned on here, so I tried to be quick.

I grabbed a blanket from the bed and curled up with my cases by the fire. I flipped through the pages quickly realizing that my first case was my only easy case. At some point I fell asleep.

I was shaken awake a short time later. "Hey, Grace, wake up." I blinked myself awake surprised to find Justin standing over me.

"Hey, I brought the cot in and made it up. You can go to bed."

I nodded, wanting to tell him to just let me sleep in the chair but when I closed my eyes again I heard him curse under his breath and scoop me up in his arms. He carried me the short distance and sat me on the fold-out cot.

"Thank you," I mumbled as I wiggled and fumbled with the blankets to crawl under them.

I heard him cross the room and pull off his clothes. I barely opened my eyes and watched as he stripped down to nothing and climbed into his own bed. I snuggled into a pillow that smelled a great deal like him. It was woodsy with a hint of spice. I sighed happily and drifted off to sleep.

Chapter Three

An alarm clock was going off somewhere in the room when I opened my eyes. I looked around the darkened chamber and quickly found the offender. I stumbled across the room to the bed that took up most of the corner. Justin was lightly snoring. I picked up his phone and noticed the time was six AM. I looked at his adorable sleeping face and hit the snooze button.

The fire had died and the floor was almost like ice even through my wool socks. I made my cot up so it looked less messy and pulled on my clothes from yesterday. Quietly as possible I ducked out the front door and headed for the bathroom and kitchen. I had been lucky enough to find a stash of new toothbrushes in the bathroom the night before and was looking forward to coffee and lack of morning breath.

When I wandered into the kitchen I found a short round woman about my height standing beside the massive oven flipping pancakes. She turned and gave me a surprised look.

"Oh, hello there. You must be Justin's little friend. You're very short for a Werewolf, aren't you?" Her smile was warm and inviting. She had a lone dimple just like Justin.

"Hi, I'm Grace." I leaned forward and shook her hand. "I'm only half Were. My mother is a bonded Human and she is shorter than I am." I smiled broadly. "Are you one of Justin's sisters?"

She flipped a pancake and laughed. It was a full-hearted, merry sound. "Heavens no. You're a sweet girl. I'm his mother, Joy. Nice to meet you, Gracie - are you hungry?"

I meant to tell her I just needed a cup of coffee but soon I was seated in the dining room with a dozen or so Dwarves eating pancakes, eggs, and bacon. All of the Dwarves took a moment to introduce themselves. For so early in the morning they were a lively bunch. They had me smiling and laughing with everyone despite the wee hours. I was just standing up to return my dishes to the kitchen when the door to the dining room was slammed open.

"You!" Justin's voice was deep and filled with deadly menace as he pointed at me.

I blinked at him. "Did I drink the last of the coffee?" I looked down at the mug in my hand.

He stormed angrily across the dining room. All the Dwarves were stunned into silence. I held out my mug. "It's got milk and sugar in it but if you want it..."

"You turned off my alarm!" he accused.

I shifted uncomfortably. "Actually I just hit snooze. You were out cold and looked so peaceful."

"I don't have a snooze," he growled.

"I didn't know that. I thought I was being helpful." I offered an apologetic smile.

Justin roared again and turned to walk away. He paused, turned back to me, took the cup of coffee, then disappeared in the direction he had come from. I finished collecting my plates in silence. Everyone was staring at me.

"Well, I hope I haven't ruined anyone else's morning, because I'm out of coffee." I laughed nervously and took my plates into the kitchen.

Checking the clock on the wall I rushed to take care of my bathroom needs and finish getting dressed. Gathering my cases, uniform, and hat in my arms I headed for the office. I got about three steps out the door and turned back to the house.

I stepped into the kitchen and smiled at Joy. "Can I make a doggie bag to take with me?" I asked.

She handed me a plastic container and pointed me to the leftovers. I stacked four pancakes, a handful of sausage, and some bacon, eggs and toast into the container. "Thank you."

She looked at the massive pile. "You'll fit in here just fine with a healthy appetite like that." I smiled as I ducked out the door.

I looked off into the distance and could see the smoke from the fireplaces in the main workshop billowing towards the sky. I pushed myself into a run to get across the icy cold campus. The wind bit at my face, making it sting. I made it to the office with ten minutes to spare.

I quickly dropped everything on my desk and grabbed the plastic container of breakfast. I did my best to make my way back to Justin's office. As I expected he was sitting behind his laptop with a cup of coffee in one hand. I knocked on the door. Without looking up he told me to come in.

"I'm really sorry about this morning," I started. His head snapped up, an angry glare still in his eyes. Without another word I tiptoed across the office and sat the breakfast container on his desk.

"Yeah, I'm going to go work now." He eyed the container with disbelief. He looked like he was going to say something but I didn't stick around long enough to be snapped at again.

I clocked in just as it snapped to eight AM. I opened the case files I had brought home with me last night to review. My next two cases dealt with matters of the heart. One was for an Elven Prince who had his heart set on a Dwarven bride. They had gotten into a massive fight a few weeks ago and she had returned to her own Kingdom. Their engagement was then broken. Now, she was engaged to another from a different Kingdom. Breaking the engagement could mean war for her people but there was the small problem that she was still in love with the Prince.

I fumbled with my pen trying to figure out how best to handle this. I wasn't very familiar with customs from other realms as I had never really left the Human realm. My father had said that other realms could be too dangerous. Sighing heavily I put the file aside and grabbed the other one.

The next case seemed like something out of Dickens. An old woman had withdrawn from the world. She lived alone with a handful of cats. *Crazy old cat lady cannot bode well for me,* I thought. While she had plenty of money, she had no kindness for others. She underpaid her personal assistant and was now making the unfortunate assistant work Christmas when she had promised her a holiday vacation. The assistant had saved for two years to afford the plane ticket home to see her family but now couldn't even get a refund.

I looked around the room. There were at least a half dozen of us who were Holiday Spirits. Some of them were pulling on uniforms while others were making phone calls. It was then I noticed they all had heavy wool coats or cloaks lined in flannel or fur. Even their gowns were made of thicker fabric. Pursing my lips I looked at my pile of thin cloth then back at the others. One after another they tossed bits of the fake snow into the air and disappeared.

The only way I was going to get to the bottom of this Elf and Dwarven dilemma was to see it firsthand. I stripped and pulled on the "uniform". The dress was strapless and laced tightly up the back. It was slit to the hip on either side. The cape attached to my wrists and the back of my dress dragged behind me on the ground. I tugged the heavy green wreath onto my head and looked in the mirror beside the door. I felt like I was dressed for a comic convention and not for spreading Yuletide cheer. When I turned around I found the few other women left in the office staring at me open-mouthed.

"It's all she had left," I offered.

"What the heck did you say to Maggie to make her give you that?" asked one Gnome. "You're going to freeze to death."

"I wish I knew." I shrugged. I picked up the case file and the magic snow. "How do I use this stuff?" I asked as I looked at it.

"Haven't you ever used magic? It's all-purpose snow," offered another woman.

"No, I've lived in the Human realm my entire life. Raised mostly Human in fact." They all exchanged looks.

"Pinch some, toss it over your head and tell it where you want to go," called out the Gnome on the phone.

I looped the bag around my wrist, opened the case file and tossed the snow in the air. "The castle of Prince Maerryn."

The air above me twinkled and I watched in amazement when the world changed shape around me. A castle came into view as blast of icy wind hit me. A chill ran through me that shot clear to my toes.

I looked around and when I saw only a few people standing about, I marched up the stone stairs to the door of what looked like the front of the castle. I knocked but nobody answered, so I pushed the door open and stepped inside.

The hall within was huge. Castle staff hustled around busily hanging greenery and tapestries on every available wall. At the center of it all stood a short woman with wavy dark hair, directing. Every time she picked something up someone would come by and take it out of her hands. I closed the door behind me.

"Excuse me," I called across the room.

Nobody answered. Taking my courage in hand I crossed to the woman at the center of the room. "Excuse me?" I said again a little louder.

The dark haired woman whirled around to face me. Her eyes flared with surprise when she saw me.

"Yes. Oh my! Who are you?" she asked. She looked at my clothes and raised a curious brow.

"I'm a Holiday Spirit, here for Prince Maerryn. Do you know where I could find him?" I asked as politely as I could.

She bent down to pick up a box of greenery but suddenly out of nowhere a tall Elf with long dark hair appeared. He grabbed the box from her hands and held it high above his head.

"I told you not to lift anything heavy." She stood on her toes reaching for it before she looked back at me.

"Oh, sorry. I'm not entirely sure where he is. I believe he is out looking for a tree for the main hall with members of the guard." She looked back at the Elf. "Tallyn, give me the damn box. I'll be fine, we just found out two weeks ago I'm pregnant. It will be months before we have to worry about me picking up something heavy," she growled.

Before I could stop myself I could hear myself saying, "Actually, you're most vulnerable to hurting the baby in the first trimester. As you get further along it becomes more dangerous for you in the sense you may pull something."

Both she and the tall Elf turned to look at me. "Sorry, force of habit. My dad is an OBGYN." I shrugged. The woman smiled broadly at me.

"You're from the Human realm!" She stuck out her hand. "Hi, I'm Lily, and this is my husband Tallyn, Maerryn's younger brother." She motioned to the Elf beside her who was staring at me slack-jawed.

"Aren't you cold?" he asked, taking my hand.

"More than you can ever imagine," I told him as I gave a slight curtsey.

"Why aren't you wearing more? It's dangerous to be out in so little," he added.

"I somehow managed to piss of a Gnome at the North Pole. Do you know where I might find your brother?" I tried to redirect attention back to my case.

"He's out getting a tree, but you can't go out there like that. You should stay here until he gets back." He turned and called a maid over. "Fetch a blanket and hot drink for our guest."

Lily stepped beside me, lacing her arm through mine and guiding me towards the fireplace. "Ca'mon, have a seat by the fire, get warm and keep me company while you wait. They aren't going to let me do anything anyway."

We settled into a couple high back chairs by the fire. The maid arrived with a thick warm blanket and two steaming cups of tea, which I gladly accepted one of. "So tell me, how do you know Maerryn?"

"Truthfully, I don't."

She paused and considered me for a moment. Her look told me she fully expected more of an explanation. Before long I had told Lily how I lost my job and ended up working at the North Pole for the season.

"And so now I'm stuck playing Holiday Spirit from now until Christmas Eve. How did you end up here?" I asked.

She gave me a friendly laugh and told me all about the powers of Soul Mates and how she and Tallyn had ended up together. I sipped on the tea, enthralled by her tale. When the doors to the great hall burst open and a tall blonde Elf strolled in barking orders I knew I had found my Prince. I thanked Lily, set down my teacup and marched across the hall.

"Prince Maerryn?" I asked as I approached. He whirled around, his face lighting up as his eyes raked over my body.

"Yes, my Lady, how can I help you?" he answered.

"Wonderful," I cried happily.

I smiled sweetly at him, stepped close, grabbed the front of his tunic in my hand, and tossed some magic snow into the air above us. "The Dwarven stronghold where I can find Lady Fairwynn." Once again the air around us began to twinkle. Maerryn fought against my grip but it was too late. He was coming with me.

When the world materialized around us we were standing in the kitchen of a great stone building. The entire kitchen staff turned to stare at us.

Maerryn yanked out of my grasp. "What's wrong with you?!?" he demanded of me.

"I'm your Holiday Spirit," I responded with a sarcastic smile.

"You're my what," he asked flatly.

"Your Holiday Spirit. I'm here to make sure you get the happy Yule you deserve with your Dwarven bride." With a soothing breath, I relaxed enough to offer a genuine smile.

"She doesn't want me," he responded.

"I have a case file that says she loves you and you love her. She's about to make a big mistake and end up with another guy, so you have to tell her how you feel or you will both be miserable for a long, long time. If you're anything like Werewolves that could be centuries." I was gasping for air by the time I finished my rant.

"Prince Maerryn!" A strong masculine voice called from behind us.

I whirled around in time to catch sight of a Dwarven man with short dark hair and playful eyes strolling towards us. "I'm glad to see you, brother. You came to your senses and are here to get my sister back." The man looked at me with confusion. "Who's that?"

"Good to see you too, James. This is my Holiday Spirit. She kidnapped me and dragged me here to make me win back your sister." Maerryn's words were laced with annoyance.

James rubbed his chin as he looked me over. "Aren't you cold?" he finally asked.

I rolled my eyes. "Yes! Very."

James called for a maid. "Girl, please fetch the lady a blanket and something warm to drink."

He turned his attention back to Maerryn. "I'm glad you're here. Fairwynn just agreed to a binding with a Werewolf noble. He's a nice enough chap, but I know she is still hung up on you. She thinks it will be good for the Kingdom if she makes a tie between the races."

Maerryn shook his head. "I'm not here to stop her. Like I said, I was kidnapped and brought here." With an angry thrust of his hand he pointed at me. "By her!" Everyone in the kitchen looked at me.

Shifting uncomfortably side to side, I looked at the heavy stone floor before looking up at Maerryn and smiling again. When I met the fury in his eyes all my confidence was gone.

"I'm just doing my job!" I whined loudly. "Give me a break, this is like day one and a half for me."

"Did I ask you to help me?" he asked angrily.

I started to answer but suddenly there was a woman's confused voice from the far side of the kitchen.

"Maerryn? What are you doing here?" I turned to find a Dwarven woman with copper hair pulled up into a large bun entering the kitchen. Her pale skin looked like porcelain against the dim lights at the door.

"Fairwynn," Maerryn choked. "I'm, ah, here..." He trailed off.

I cleared my throat. "He's here to see you." I filled in.

She turned to look at me. She opened her mouth to ask something but I quickly interjected. "Yes, I'm cold and someone is already getting me a drink and blanket, thank you."

She snapped her mouth shut and looked at Maerryn and James.

"Who is she?" she asked.

"Our Holiday Spirit. She's here to assure you and I have a merry Yule and end up together," Maerryn responded.

I shrugged and nodded when she looked back at me. Fairwynn was silent for a moment then rushed forward, throwing her arms around Maerryn.

"I missed you so much! I'm sorry," she said as she buried her face into his tunic.

Giving up he wrapped his arms around her and started offering apologies as well. "I'm sorry. I shouldn't have gotten so mad at you. I just don't want you in harm's way," he said, tucking a loose strand of her hair behind an ear.

James appeared at my side. "My Lady, why don't we clear out and give them some room." I looked back at the couple then allowed James to escort me into a great hall where a large number of castle staff were also decorating.

"I bet this place is beautiful when it's all decorated." I stared at all the intricate stonework.

"It is," he answered. "So do you know many of the Dwarves at the North Pole?" he asked.

"Only a few. I just arrived yesterday. I met Justin Kringle. He's sort of grumpy but every so often I see this glimpse of something charming and sweet. I also met his mother Joy this morning and a few of his sisters and cousins."

I smiled, remembering breakfast. Within minutes I had felt like a member of the family. "They seem like really good people."

"They are. The Kringles were originally from this realm. A great number of the Dwarves here will head to the North Pole to help out a week or two before Yule." He smiled. "I go almost every year. It's become a tradition for my sister and me."

I accepted a hot mug of something alcoholic when it was handed to me. "Thank you!" I said, smiling at the maid that brought it. I took a sip and it burned all the way down but tasted amazing. "Wow, this is amazing."

James laughed. "I'll give you a small keg to take back if you can help solve the rest of the problem."

I looked at him, processing his words. "The rest of the problem?"

He pointed to a tall muscular man with grey eyes that seemed to glow a little in the shadows where he sat reading.

"The Werewolf that my sister just agreed to marry. While we've had a peaceful existence with them, this union would do a lot to improve trade. There is also a good chance that cancelling the binding could cause a war."

I took another deep swig of the hot drink. Just then I watched Fairwynn and Maerryn approach him. I swallowed hard.

"You should get over there. If they about to do what I think they are..." My words died as the man sprang to his feet and started yelling. James ran towards the group but by the time he arrived Maerryn was drawing his sword.

I slammed down what was left of the drink and placed the cup on the table beside me. I could already feel my cheeks growing pink. *That was one strong drink,* I thought to myself as I crossed the hall to join the brawl.

"You can't just cancel a binding contract," yelled the Were.

"Micholie, I love this Elf," Fairwynn argued.

I processed the name as the continued to argue. Micholie was threatening war and shame for the dishonor. Maerryn was threatening the same if he didn't stand down.

"Micholie Duncan?" I asked quirking my head to the side, staring at him wide-eyed.

The Were froze and turned to face me. "Aye, My Lady?"

I burst into a fit of giggles. He stared at me like I had snakes growing out of my head... or maybe just a wreath.

"Micholie Duncan, you had a crush for the longest time on my cousin Lana. She used to tell me millions of stories about you when I would visit in the summer." I started giggling again. "Like the time you tried to pee on an elec-" The large Were clamped a hand over my mouth.

"Lana's cousin? Just who are you, My Lady?" His voice was harsh.

Grinning with what I could already feel was a slightly drunk grin I said, "Gracie MacGregor," and giggled again.

"A relation of Cariss MacGregor then?" he asked, his tone changing.

"Yeah, that's my father's older brother," I answered. I was swaying a little under the intoxication.

Micholie reached out to steady me. "Yer Arjin's lass?" There was a slight grin on his face.

"Yesh," I responded with another giggle.

"He couldna hold his Dwarven brews either. How-ja end up here, girl?" He looked at what I was wearing. "In that?"

I laughed. "I lost my job so I took a gig at the North Pole. I'm a Holiday Spirit," I said with a nod. Before long we were seated by the fire chatting and drinking, comparing notes about the family.

Fairwynn approached a little later to try and talk to Micholie again. When she interrupted he cut her off. "Yeah, yeah, true love, I'm happy for ya, Lass. Canya not see I'm talkin to my kin?"

"What are you doing for the holidays?" I asked.

He shrugged. "I thought about goin to Human realm and visiting Scotland's clan lands."

"Ah, don't do that. They're all crossing the pond to my parents this year. There are going to be like fifty Were there from the day before Yule to New Years. Go to my parents'," I offered.

"Will that be alright?" he asked, surprised.

"Yeah, Mom is all about the more the merrier. I'll shoot her an email tonight and let her know you're coming." We talked for a few more minutes and then exchanged the standard big hug.

When I crossed back over to James, Maerryn, and Fairwynn, they were all staring at me wide-eyed.

"You're a Werewolf?" James asked.

I shrugged. "Only half."

Maerryn stepped forward. "Well I certainly can't thank you enough. Is there anything I can do to return the favor?" he asked.

"Have a happy holiday so I don't have to come back," I smiled.

Before I left, James had a large wooden keg of Dwarven Holiday Brew brought out for me. I thanked him again then tossed a little fake snow into the air while touching the keg. "Joy's kitchen at the North Pole." With a familiar twinkle the world melted around me.

Chapter Four

When everything came back into focus Joy was cooking at the stove. "Hi Joy!" I piped up.

She jumped with a little squeak and whirled around. She eyed me where I sat on top of the keg with my feet dangling.

"What are you wearing, dear, and where did that come from?" she asked motioning towards the keg.

I hiccupped. "The Great Dwarven Stronghold gave it to me for preventing a war."

I looked down at my dress noticing I really could see right through it. "And this is the Holiday Spirit uniform Maggie assigned me."

Joy pursed her lips together for a moment. "What did you say to Maggie?" she asked.

I laughed. "I don't know. I just walked in with Justin and this is what I got."

"Oh," said Joy.

"Oh?" I asked.

She smiled mischievously. "She has a little crush on my boy. He doesn't normally help the new recruits with things like uniforms. She must have thought something was going on."

I shook my head. "Boy did she read it wrong. It couldn't be further from the truth. Justin tolerates me at best." I laughed a little, thinking about this morning's exchange.

She chuckled. "He can be a little rough around the edges because he takes his job very seriously. I promise you, he's a teddy bear."

"Even so, I still think I'll take my chances with the wolves." I looked at the clock. It was nearly nine in the evening. "Do you need help cleaning up from dinner? I can go change and come back and give you a hand," I offered.

"That's sweet of you, but I'll be alright. How were the leftovers for lunch?" she asked.

"What leftovers?" I asked.

"The ones from breakfast you took with you this morning." She glanced at me.

"Oh, no. I took those to Justin. He missed breakfast because of me so I wanted to make sure he had food to start the day with." Just then my stomach rumbled.

"Did you eat lunch or dinner?" she asked me, eyeing my noisy belly.

"No, I was really busy today and just lost track of time. I did have a cup of tea and a mug of this stuff." I bounced on the keg to prove a point.

"That's not food. If you keep not eating and running around in next to nothing you'll end up sick." She turned and pulled out a tray. Immediately she began filling it with leftovers. She poured boiling water in a teapot as well then handed me the whole tray. "Just bring me back the dishes when you're done."

"You didn't need to do all that. I would have been fine making a cup of tea and a bowl of cereal or toast for myself." I smiled down at the food.

She rolled her eyes. "I don't know why you haven't wasted away if that's how you normally eat. Now go get warmed up and eat something. Not another word." Following orders I left the keg in the kitchen and marched across the cold threshold into Justin's quarters.

He was sitting in his chair by the fire reading when I came in. I walked across the room and sat the tray on the small table. He looked up from his book to say something and froze, his eyes large. "What are you wearing?" he asked, standing up from the chair.

"The uniform Maggie gave me. Remember, you were there," I offered. He crossed the short distance between us, tugging the blanket off the back of the chair as he came. In a fluid motion he swung it around me and began rubbing my arms and shoulders.

"You've been out all day in only this?" I wasn't sure he really meant for me to answer the question. I nodded.

Reaching under the blanket ran his hands up and down my sides. "Your whole body is like ice." His words were soft. He rested his hands on my bare thighs where the fabric split at the hips. "Didn't you notice you were cold?"

"Only up until they started making me drink at the Dwarven Stronghold. Then I didn't really notice or care anymore." I smirked.

"They saw you? You were drinking on the job?" The softness in his voice was gone. Now it was a mix of shock and annoyance.

"Yes, of course they did. I helped an Elven Prince and Dwarven Lady come together because they were in love. Then I prevented a war between the Werewolves and Dwarves. They were so happy they insisted I bring back a keg of Holiday Brew." His jaw dropped.

"You talked to them?" He sounded mad, really mad. "Holiday Spirits aren't supposed to be seen and certainly not heard.

"If they hadn't heard me there would have been a war." I wasn't going to let him just stand here and yell at me.

"Your job is Holiday Spirit. You are not supposed to talk to any of your cases." He turned angrily on his heel and went to stand and look out the window.

"Actually, it doesn't say in the contract I can't talk to cases." I watched him stiffen. "You implied it when you talked about what I was wearing, but you never said it was an official rule."

I pulled the wreath off of my head, then unlaced the dress, letting it and the cape drop to the floor. I was just reaching for the flannel shirt I had worn the night before when he whirled around to face me. He stood there gaping. "If it's not in my contract and you didn't forbid me from doing it you really can't be mad at me." I tugged the shirt on, leaving the top few buttons undone.

Justin shook his head. "I don't remember telling you that it was ok to borrow my clothes," he snapped.

I blushed because I knew I was in the wrong. "I'm sorry, I just thought you would be more comfortable with me sleeping in this rather than nude." I started to grab the hem.

"No!" he said loudly. "That's alright, you can borrow it. Just ask next time, alright?" I nodded.

He looked over at the table. "If you're going to eat you should do it soon. That seems like an awful big snack," he teased.

"Would you like some?" I offered as I sat down on the ottoman. He came to sit in the chair beside me, tossing the blanket back around my shoulders before sitting down.

Between bites we actually talked. I asked about his day and he replied cheerfully. "Did you find the food court alright?" he asked, popping the last bite of bread in his mouth.

"No," I said, sipping on the now lukewarm tea.

"Didn't anyone show you where it was?" he asked with concern.

"No, I was out in the field preventing a war all day, remember? When I came in a little bit ago I was just getting back." I took the last sip of tea.

"You were out all day in that dress?" He was really starting to sound upset.

"Yes, you gave me a job to do. I may not do it the way you think I should but I've never had my work ethic called into question." I didn't mean to get upset.

"Shhh shh." He rubbed my back through the blanket. "I wasn't accusing you of anything. I was merely stunned. So if you were in the field all day..." He looked at the tray of food we just ate. "You didn't eat lunch or dinner, did you?"

I shook my head. "No, I didn't have time."

He sighed. "Why didn't you say that was your dinner?"

"There was enough to share." I started to stand with the intention of returning the dishes.

He quickly stood up and took the tray. "I've got it. Would you like more tea?" he offered.

Shaking my head I smiled. "No, I'm alright. Is there any way I could send an email though? I should let my parents know where I am and what I'm doing. My mother is a worrywart."

Justin took a step towards the door. "Sure, my tablet is on the bed. You're welcome to use that. The whole Pole is wired for Wifi. I'll be back in a few." He disappeared out the front door.

I walked over to the bed and began looking for the tablet. When I finally found it, it was under a thick fur-lined quilt. I lay flat on my stomach, noticing I couldn't stretch the full length of the bed. I smiled, thinking Dwarves must move around a lot in their sleep. I flipped the electronic on and it glowed to life.

I quickly shot Mom an email letting her know about my seasonal job and where I was. I also made sure to mention Micholie coming for the holidays. I knew she wouldn't mind, but I also knew she disliked surprises as much as I did. When I finished, I perused my favorite social network sites and even peeked at eBay for some holiday shopping. I was amazed that it was taking Justin so long to get back, but then maybe he was spending time with the family. I shrugged it off. Just as I was placing a bid on a sweater the door burst open.

"Grace, I brought you..." Justin looked at the chair by the fire and confusion crossed his face. He scanned the room and found me draped across the bed looking at the tablet. I immediately started to get up.

"No, you don't have to move." He kicked the door shut and his shoes off and came across the room with two mugs of hot brew. "Sorry, they were cracking it open, then it needed to be heated and it's not right everyone else was drinking it without you enjoying some too." I sat up and happily accepted the mug.

"This mug is much larger than the one I had today at the Stronghold," I laughed. It must have been three times the size.

"It's because it gets much colder here. We want to make sure we don't have to leave the warmth of the fire to refill as often," he joked.

I took a big sip and enjoyed the feeling of it burning down my throat. By halfway through the mug I was well past tipsy and by the end I was totally drunk. We talked about family, work and life.

"When I was twelve my parents finally sat me down and explained what we were. I was really confused."

"I bet. I would be too." Justin was an amazing listener when he was drinking.

"I told my Dad it didn't matter as long as I didn't have to shave four times a day." We both laughed. A shiver ran through me.

"Are you cold?" he asked.

"Just a little," I mentioned, going back to the story. He shifted on the bed, tugging me to lean against him. He then pulled several of the blankets up around us. We continued telling stories and laughing well into the wee hours of the morning.

When the alarm started buzzing I begrudgingly opened my eyes. I realized I was very warm and the outside of the cot was very cold. I put my head back down and snuggled into my pillows. They flexed around me, pulling me closer. I felt a movement and the alarm stopped making noise. I blinked my eyes open. I was still in bed with Justin.

I tried to tell myself not to panic. I started to sit up, but he pulled me back down. In a half dazed sleep-filled voice he whispered, "If we skip breakfast and take a snowmobile we don't have to get up for another hour." I eyed him closely.

"I need a shower," I whispered.

As if to prove a point he smelled my hair. "You still smell like a girl. You're fine." I started to try and get up, but the hangover hit me and I fell back against the pillows.

"Hangover?" he asked.

"Yes," I answered.

"See, it's the Pole's way of saying you should sleep another hour." He snuggled closer. Giving up, I closed my eyes and dozed another hour.

Chapter Five

When the alarm sounded again we both opened our eyes and exchanged looks that said we needed at least another three hours of sleep. "Ready to get up?" asked Justin in a husky voice.

"No, but I don't really have a choice." We both grumbled and climbed out of bed. "I have an hour, right?" I asked to clarify. He nodded. "I'll meet you by the front door in thirty minutes." I rushed to the closet, tugged out a clean change of clothes, and ran out the front door and to the bathrooms. I went to three bathrooms before finding a shower that was free. I did a quick wash, brushed my teeth, and yanked on clothes.

As I hit the kitchen I smiled at Joy and asked if she had a couple portable mugs I could borrow. When she pointed me to the cabinet I made haste to grab a couple and fill them with coffee, milk and sugar, then dashed from the kitchen with a thank you. I heard her chuckling as I left.

I was at the front door just as Justin tugged it open. He handed me a bag as he stepped out into the cold. "I thought you may want your magic and uniform."

"Thank you," I said as I handed him the travel mug full of coffee.

"What's this?" he asked, eyeing the mug.

"Coffee," I replied with a shrug. "I don't know about you but I'm considered a lethal driver without it in the morning." I tugged the bag over my shoulder.

"About last night."

I cut him off. "We can't tell anyone or they may get the wrong idea." He nodded. "I know," I smiled back at him.

We walked in silence to the snowmobiles. "Do you want to drive?" A smile tugged at his mouth.

I winced. "I'm not sure that's a good idea. I haven't finished my first cup yet." We laughed but he took the bag from my shoulder and flung it over his. He quickly finished his coffee and tucked the empty mug in the bag.

I climbed on, listening closely as he explained the controls to me. He then climbed on behind me, tucking his arms around my waist and pulling me back against him, cradled between his thighs. Even through my coat it felt nice to be pressed against him, but I wasn't about to tell him that. Soon we were off whizzing over the frozen ground towards the workshop. I pulled off the path like we had a few days before and parked with the others snowmobiles hidden just out of sight.

Taking the bag and my coffee back I smiled. "Thanks for the lesson."

"Anytime. Actually, I usually leave around six. Meet me here and we can ride back together." His offer was compelling.

"I'll do my best." I turned to head into the office. Luck was on my side and I arrived at five till eight.

When I arrived, my desk was buried under a mountain of case files. I looked around the office but everyone seemed preoccupied.

"Does anyone know why it snowed cases?" I asked the Spirits around me. Keeping my gaze even, I scanned each office inhabitant - no one would even make eye contact with me.

"Oh, I see how this game is going to work," I muttered.

I spent the next two hours sorting and stacking the cases on my desk. When I finished, I had sorted what I figured were 'easily dealt with', 'lots of footwork' and 'might require an army' piles. I opened the first of the 'footwork' cases and read through it in more detail.

There was a group of Dragons which had had an ancient artifact stolen earlier this year. They were unable to locate the artifact. It was important because it was linked to an ancient Yule tradition where they passed their Dragon fire on to villages so they would have heat and light through the long winter. This tradition represented the agreement between the Dragons and villages that the villagers could live in peace without fear.

I dug through the "easy" cases, positive I had seen another assignment in that realm. Sure enough, there was a local artisan that had been recently injured and was unable to work. His business had suffered greatly and now he was worried about being able to provide for his family through the winter. I thought of my co-workers back in Portland who were now facing similar worries for their own families.

I clipped the two cases together with the intention of resolving them at the same time. I would address them after lunch. I picked up another of the easy cases from the corner of my desk. This one had caught my eye because it involved my cousin Ian. He was trying to figure out how to convince the new girlfriend to come home with him for the holidays.

It made me laugh because I knew just how intimidating our family functions could be. It was more distressing that the next Chieftain was afraid to bring his new girl home, though. I knew this would be a phone call. I looked at my clock and realized two things. The first was that it was lunch time. The second was that I had no clue what time zone I was in and so had no way to know what time it was in Asia.

With a happy sigh I shoved myself back from my desk and set out on a mission to find the cafeteria. I looked pointedly as a Gnome who was sitting at her desk playing a game on her computer.

"Where is the cafeteria?" I asked, plastering on my best new girl smile.

She looked up at me in surprise. "Huh?"

"Where is the cafeteria where I can get some food?" I motioned like I was eating something.

"Oh!" she said and glanced down at the clock. "It's lunchtime! Follow me and I'll show you." She hopped off her chair and walked by me quickly.

I had to jog a few steps to catch up. I walked with her down a corridor and past a few turns. She pushed open two large red swinging doors that revealed a massive cafeteria. It looked like it belonged on the top floor of an expensive department store. Holiday decorations covered every corner, mixed with retro furniture made of bright colors and chrome.

"So if you go get in line over there you can pick out what you want for lunch, then you pay over there." My gaze followed her hand as she pointed out the key locations.

Her smiling face was a welcome change from the few encounters I had experienced so far with the other Spirits. I realized she said pay and I froze. I didn't have any money or credit cards with me.

I cursed under my breath and she looked at me, startled. "Sorry. I didn't mean to offend you," I quickly apologized.

She laughed, a full hearted chortle. "Oh, you didn't. You just don't hear people talk like that much up here. It caught me by surprise, that's all. What's up?"

I rolled my eyes and smiled widely. "When they zapped me up here to start working I didn't have a chance to grab my purse, credit cards or anything."

"I can see why that could be a problem. Why not use the all-purpose snow and pop home to get your belongings?" I stared at her in amazement. Why hadn't I thought of that?

"That's brilliant!" I turned to go back to the office and grab the snow. Her next words stopped me. "Just don't get caught."

I spun around to face her. "What do you mean?"

"Just what I said. Don't get caught. Spirits are forbidden from using their magic for personal gain." The words from the contract suddenly rang a familiar tune.

She looked left and right, then leaned close to me. "But everyone does it."

I considered her words for a moment. I had never really been a massive rule breaker, so the idea of breaking one now didn't sit well with me. "Can I ask HR permission?"

She thought about it a moment. "You could, but Helen's on maternity leave until after first of the year.

I believe that Justin is covering HR for her while she is out."

"Ah, I thought he was HR. What is his normal title?" I was really curious now. Maybe he had played up his newfound power.

"Chief Operations Officer," she replied matter-of-factly. "You'll want to set up an appointment with his secretary to discuss it."

"Thanks... I just realized I don't know your name?" I could feel myself blushing brightly.

"Mary. And your name is Grace, right?" She reached out, taking my hand in a firm shake. "Well, I'm going to go grab a quick bite." She turned and disappeared into the crowd.

My stomach rumbled angrily. I left the cafeteria and headed back to the office. Lunch was nearly over anyway. Maybe I would get lucky and the Dragons would feed me. Dad always said they were pretty hospitable.

I dressed and poofed across realms just as the other Spirits were returning from their lunches. I managed to catch a few more stares from them, as they looked over my less-than-traditional uniform. I suppose it could have been worse. It could have been red.

The biting cold wind hit me full force as I materialized in the realm of Dragons. It whipped my dress around me and threatened to blow the ugly wreath off my head. For a split second I wished it would, until I remembered they would charge me if I didn't return it. Clamping a hand on it tightly, I took a moment to look around.

There was nobody in sight. There was no village, no Dragons and no heat source to be seen. I was about to reach for my all-purpose snow when I heard laughter above me. I looked up just in time to see two large Dragons swoop down and disappear into the side of the cliff.

"Hey!" I yelled loudly up the face of the cliff. "Down here!" I waved my arms frantically. *Maybe I should dye the dress red after all. A white dress in a snow storm does nothing to help me.*

I heard the crunch of snow behind me and whirled to see who was there. To my horror and surprise a large Dragon with golden eyes stretched to his full height. Spreading his wings wide he let out a loud screech. I did what any woman in the face of such a danger would do. I screamed and turn to run away.

"Dad, you're such a liar. Friendly and hospitable my ass," I cursed as I crunched through the snow. I only made it a few steps when two taloned claws wrapped around my arms and lifted me from the ground.

As I prepared to scream again I was set down on the floor of a cave up the side of the cliff's face. Before me stood two naked men. I turned in time to watch the dragon who had carried me up morph into his Human form as well. The only signs that indicated they were Dragons were their eyes and a slight shimmering scale pattern to their skin.

"Ummmm, hi." I was meeting Dragons for the first time and that's all I could come up with.

The shortest of the three stepped forward with a boyish smile. "Sorry about scaring you but you seemed like you wanted to get our attention."

He held out his hand. "Hello, I'm Lord Geren and these are the Lords Hudraer and Vallen." I looked from the golden man to the dark haired one and nodded.

"I'm Grace, your Holiday Spirit. I've come to assist you with the missing artifact. I want to help you locate it." I smiled brightly and took the hand that was offered.

The three exchanged glances before looking back at me. "Grace, how exactly do you know about the artifact that's missing?" asked Lord Vallen.

"Well it's in my case file, so I guess someone at the OAC knows about it." I stopped and worked through what I was saying. "They knew when I lost my job almost before I did. That's how they roped me into this gig."

The three of them were dressing quickly around me, speaking a language I wasn't familiar with. Finally Geren spoke up. "So you're with the OAC?"

"No, I'm part of Holiday operations. I guess that's a sub-department of the OAC. I'm afraid I'm not the best at this. I'm really new." I shrugged and stepped closer to a torch, hoping its warmth would penetrate the icy chill that was running through me.

"New? Like, less than one hundred years?" Geren asked tentatively.

"New, like this week," I answered with a nod.

Vallen cut in. "Don't take this the wrong way, but we can't figure it out and we're Dragons who have been hunting treasure our entire lives. Forgive us if we don't really understand why we need you."

I fisted my hands tight and bit back the little bit of anger. "Obviously, the OAC believes you need my help or they wouldn't have given me your case file. I'll have you know I prevented a war yesterday afternoon in the realm of the Four Kingdoms." I crossed my arms over my chest to signal I wasn't going anywhere.

"Aren't you cold?" Lord Hudraer finally asked.

"Absolutely frozen," I responded in a flat tone.

"You could catch your death out there dressed like that. It doesn't show good sense at all," said Vallen. He then stepped forward, lifted his cloak from the ground nearby, and swept it around my shoulders.

I wanted to be mad at him. His directness stung at my pride a little. "It's my uniform. I evidentially made the mistake of walking into the uniform department with the wrong person and was assigned this get-up as a cruel joke. I get to wear it every day for the next three weeks," I finished with a sarcastic tone.

Lord Vallen smiled and even chuckled. "I'm sorry to make light of it when it so obviously bothers you." When he smiled, he was just as handsome as the other two. I had heard many a story of men and women falling for Dragons because of their striking otherworldly beauty. I now understood why.

I shook my head as if to rattle the marbles back in place. "I swear I can be of help if you let me." I held up three fingers giving the Girl Scout promise and realized they had no clue what I was doing.

"Wait right here," said Geren. He and the others stepped away and talked for a moment before returning. "Ok, follow us, but stay close."

I did as I was told and was led down into the heart of their lair to a large main room. There were many Dragons of all ages around. Lord Hudraer stepped forward and quieted the questions.

"This is Grace. She is a Holiday Spirit assigned by the OAC to help us with the missing artifact. If she asks you for any help please be respectful and do your best to assist her." He then turned to two young boys playing nearby. "Go get our guest a hot drink and some food." The boys ran off immediately to fulfill his request.

Soon I was seated at the table, warm and munching on sweetbreads as I got all the details. After I heard the whole story I contemplated it carefully. "Don't Dragons have vaults and stuff to keep their treasure safe?"

"Of course we do," responded Lord Geren.

"Then is it safe to say the only people who could get in without you noticing would be another Dragon?" I took a sip of the hot mulled wine they had been kind enough to provide me with.

The exchanged glances told me they had already considered this possibility. "Do you have any suspects?"

"None," answered Lord Vallen. "No one here would steal from the clans. The artifact is important to us all. We've spoken with all the men and women and no one knows anything."

I considered his words. "What about the kids?"

"The children? They wouldn't know anything about it." He seemed so sure but I, having actually been a child within the last hundred years, remembered just how much I always knew.

"I'm not saying they're at fault, but often children have seen something and no one thinks to ask them." I leaned back in my chair and pulled the cloak tighter around my shoulders.

Lord Vallen stood and called all the boys and girls over. I watched quietly as the three Lords stood over them, prodding for information. I bit back my criticism and wasn't at all surprised when I found that the children shied away from them. After they finished and the children scattered in fear I let them explain to me how the kids had nothing to add.

"Would you mind if I spoke with them?"

Vallen shrugged and Geren gave me the go ahead. I separated from the group of adults and one or two at a time spoke with each child. I came to a little boy and girl that looked like they were no more than seven or eight. Each had rust colored hair with matching green eyes.

"Are you two brother and sister?" I asked as I sat down on the floor beside them.

The boy eyed me suspiciously and stepped protectively in front of the girl. "We're twins," he barked gruffly.

"Oh, are you a good protector? Do you take care of your sister?" I asked.

"Yes, because I'm a Dragon warrior," he growled, holding up his hands like claws.

I fought the urge to laugh. "My brothers did an excellent job protecting me when I was little too," I smiled.

"But you're not a Dragon," he said. "Dragons are fierce guardians."

I nodded my head in agreement. "You're right. Dragons are fierce guardians. I'm a Werewolf. Wolves are fierce protectors too." I growled back at him. He giggled.

The little girl stepped around him. "I'm Emma, I'm a fierce Dragon too," she smiled. "This is my brother Evan. What's your name?" she asked.

"My name is Gracie. Do you and your brother help take care of all the grown-ups here?" They both vigorously agreed. "Can you help me?" I asked.

Evan pounded his fist against his chest. "We are Dragons of honor. Of course we would help a friend of the clan."

I smiled widely. "Oh thank you so much, Lord Evan and Lady Emma of the Dragons." Both their little chests puffed with pride.

"I was sent here from the North Pole because a very important Dragon artifact went missing. Your grown-ups are really worried about it. Did either of you see it recently?"

Emma played with her hands nervously. "Well..."

Evan cut her off. "Shh, Emma you can't tell."

Emma turned angrily on her brother. "Dragons are honorable and we don't tell lies." She sighed heavily. "Promise you won't be mad?"

"I promise." I shook her hand for a good measure.

"Well, we were just playing." She stopped and bit her lip. "It was an accident but we were playing hide and seek and maybe broke it."

Evan's eyes welled up with tears. "I'm sorry, be mad at me. Don't punish my sister."

I reached forward and wiped away his tears. "Nobody is going to punish you. I won't let them."

The boy wrapped his hands around my neck and hugged me. "But the elders are really scary. Won't you be scared? What if they eat you?"

I glanced around the room. Everyone seemed to be ignoring us. "I told you I was a Werewolf, right?" They both nodded. "Dragons can't eat Werewolves, we'll give them tummy aches. Besides, I have Holiday magic." I held up my wrist to show them.

"Can you show me where the relic is?"

I started to stand but Evan wouldn't let go - he was too worried. I picked him up, balancing him on a hip and hoping my dress stayed up. Emma took my other hand and led me through a series of rooms and tunnels. When we arrived she closed the door quickly behind us.

"It's in here!" She raced over to a set of shelves and pointed.

Hidden behind the shelves was a pile of broken glass, gold and jewels. I knelt, setting Evan on the floor. "Ok. Don't touch anything, I don't want you to get hurt." Grabbing the hem of my dress I gathered all the bits and pieces into it. "Is that all of it?"

Emma and Evan looked carefully and nodded. "What are you going to do now?" asked the boy.

"I'm going to fix it." Pinching a bit of the all-purpose snow I tossed it on what looked like a broken lantern. "Restore this artifact to its original form." Nothing happened. I tried again. "That's weird. Well, I guess I'll just have to find someone to fix it. Come with me."

I started to turn and walk towards the door. "Wait!" screamed Emma. "You can't show it to them broken. They'll eat us."

"I promise I won't let them eat you." I pulled the door open and hoped I could remember my way out. I took a few wrong turns that the twins were nice enough to point out. When we made it back to the main hall, they both hid behind me, tightly pressed against my thighs.

I walked to the main table where the three Lords sat talking and emptied the contents of my dress. "Is this the missing lantern?"

Lord Vallen looked pale. Lord Geren started to rise, anger rushing to his face. Lord Hudraer sat motionless, watching. "My Lords, calm down. There was an accident with the children. Nobody was hurt, but the artifact was damaged."

"This is unacceptable," raged Lord Geren. "That artifact has been a sacred piece of our history for two thousand years. There must be a punishment for such actions."

I straightened myself to my full height, which was still a head shorter than he was. "You will do no such thing!"

"You dare question me?!?" His handsome boyish face was now absolutely red.

"I do dare, and if you don't watch your tone and calm down I'll make you eat a fistful of all-purpose snow AND this stupid wreath I'm wearing."

Lord Hudraer bit off a snicker. Geren turned and glared at him before turning his wrath on me. A waft of smoke actually puffed out his nose. "I am an Elder in this clan. A Human may not understand what that means but-"

I cut him off. I allowed my inner nature to flare and felt my eyes shift. "I, as a member of clan McGregor, understand all too well. I also know that Dragons, while fierce guardians, are honorable. An honorable Dragon would never take his anger out on a child. Would he?" I heard Vallen suck in a deep breath.

My words seemed to do the trick. Lord Geren peered at the twins pressed tightly at my sides with their faces buried and instantly began to return to his normal color. "You're right. I let my temper get the better of me. Evan and Emma, you have nothing to fear. I swear it." Two little faces popped out to step beside me.

Emma put her hands on her hips. "And you should say sorry to Lady Grace. You were being a big old hot head!"

Lord Geren laughed uncomfortably and met my gaze. "I'm sorry, Grace. You came here to help and I shouldn't have been rude to you either. Is there any chance your magic can fix the lantern?"

I looked at Lord Vallen and Lord Hudraer and winced before meeting his gaze. "I tried twice already with no luck."

Hudraer stood. "Well you at least did what you came here for, which was to help us find it. For that we are truly grateful."

"I'm sorry I didn't get it back in one piece," I offered, then stopped suddenly. I reached into the front of my dress and pulled out a folded piece of paper.

"Wait, I think there is a good reason I can't fix it." I read the information on the artisan that had been injured. "Can I get a ride to the village of Maht? Also, you may want to bring your wallets."

The Dragons exchanged looks but I showed them the paper I held from the case file. I had brought the info pages with me just in case I couldn't find the location. Lord Vallen smiled, taking the paper from me.

"I see. I will go fetch a pouch to carry this in and my purse." I snickered, picturing him carrying the latest Kate Spade bag. When he returned I realized by "purse" he meant a bag of coins.

Saying my goodbyes, including a hug from each of the twins, we made our way back out to the cave entrance. He stripped naked and handed me his clothes. I watched with intrigue as he shifted into a Dragon form that looked black at first glance, but when the torchlight caught him he almost looked blue. I didn't struggle when he clutched me to make the journey.

With the freezing wind whipping by, I had lost feeling in my arms and legs by the time we landed. I handed him his clothes and he quickly redressed. It didn't take much time for us to locate the shop we needed.

The haggling that followed went quickly. The Dragons agreed to pay the artisan handsomely if he could have the lantern repaired by three days before Yule. The deal was struck, money changed hands, and all was well. Two cases for the price of one, and an ancient lantern was repaired.

I walked back to the edge of town with Lord Vallen. "Thank you for your help. I apologize for Geren's outburst. The fact that the twins are his brother and sister made him a little touchier."

"It's all in a day's work," I smiled.

"What will you do now?" He accepted the cloak as I handed it back to him.

"I will return back to the North Pole, eat some dinner, take a shower and go to bed." I laughed because it sounded strangely normal.

"If you are free on Yule we would be honored if you joined us," he said with a bow.

"It's a kind offer but I don't know what my schedule will look like at that point. I'll keep it in mind though." I offered him one last smile, tossing magic snow into the air. "Take me back to the office." I watched as the world twinkled and shifted around me.

Chapter Six

The office slid back into view. My clothes were sitting on my desk where I had left them along with piles of cases. Everyone was gone for the day. I looked at the clock and winced because it was already six fifteen. I put the case files away, grabbed my clothes and bolted out the door. I got to the snowmobiles just as Justin was starting his up.

"Sorry, I ran late!" I called.

He sighed and turned around. "I thought maybe you finished early and went back without me."

He looked me over, still standing there in my uniform. He pulled off his coat and held it open for me to put on. "Come on, let's get you back to the house and warmed up." I didn't argue. I just slid my arms into the coat and straddled the snowmobile behind him. We arrived at the house in record time.

He practically carried me to the door in an effort to get me someplace warm. "You're turning blue. We need to get you warmed up. Sit down by the fire." Before I knew it I was under a pile of blankets and furs. "Stay here, I'm going to go get tea and a first aid kit."

"A first aid kit?" I was confused until he pointed to my shoulders. I looked at one of them and noticed cuts from Lord Vallen's claws. They weren't deep and weren't bleeding any longer, but it looked like they were frozen shut.

"Hmmmm, yeah, you're probably right."

A few minutes later Justin reappeared with a tray bearing a teapot, cups, and cookies. There was also a white box with the familiar Red Cross symbol on it. I reached for the table and he shooed me away.

"Stop moving, you may make those cuts reopen. Tomorrow morning we'll need to fill out an accident report as well."

I rolled my eyes. "It's not that bad. A little ointment and some bandages."

"We still have to file the report. The rules are there for a reason." His hands were warm on my skin as he cleaned the cuts, then treated and bandaged them up. "Are you going to tell me how you got them?"

"A Dragon gave me a ride to the village. That would be my guess." I ignored him shaking his head.

"What did I tell you about being seen?" There was exasperation in his voice.

"Anyway, I'm starved so how about we change clothes and go get some food?" I smiled. Climbing out from under the blankets I tugged off the "uniform" and pulled my clothes on. Justin pretended to read something on his tablet as I carelessly changed clothes in front of him again.

When I was done he stared at me for a long moment before saying anything. "You look really pale and still sort of frozen. Do you feel alright?"

A spark of anger flared inside me but I didn't say anything. I just drank a cup of tea then made my way to the door. He motioned me to go on without him so I didn't waste time.

My stomach growled at me for my recent lack of a regular eating schedule. As I sat around the long table surrounded by Dwarves, Gnomes and a few odd Elves I started to feel a little out of place. I suddenly didn't feel like eating despite my hunger. When Justin sat down beside me I leaned over towards him.

"So I get that the Dwarves are family, who are the Gnomes and Elves?"

"They are family by marriage. Not all my cousins chose Dwarves as their mates." He smiled and filled my plate with food.

I realized the awkward feeling I got was that I was sitting here with Justin and I didn't belong at the table. Tonight felt different than breakfast had.

He looked over at me again. "Seriously, you don't look well. I brought a towel and the shirt you've been sleeping in. Why don't you go take a hot bath and I'll bring a plate of food back to the room for you to eat there?" His words were mixed with a tenderness I hadn't seen from him before. When I stood up and my head felt a little light, I agreed and made an exit for the bathroom.

When I returned to the room he had brought food back for us both and sat on the ottoman waiting for me. "Have a seat, get some food in your stomach and then you can get some sleep. Tomorrow, after the accident report, we'll go get you a proper uniform. I can't take the chance that you'll get sick so close to the Holidays."

Somehow his words stung just a little. Of course he was concerned about me. If I wasn't working it meant that things may not get done or others would have to pick up the slack. "I finished cases three and four today."

He smiled. "Wow, you're making good time. At this rate you'll finish your quota in no time."

"Yeah, it was weird though. When I got in this morning there was a mountain of cases on my desk. Some were backlogged years." I took a bite of the potatoes. After a few bites I was full. I knew I should have eaten more but I just wasn't hungry.

"That can't be right. We don't normally give more than a few cases at a time." He looked perplexed. His gaze settled on my uneaten food. "Are you done already?"

I nodded. "Yeah, I guess I am. I think I'm going to call it for the night." I moved to the cot, sinking into it and the pillow quickly.

***

I was lost, running through a forest. I kept calling for someone to hear me but nobody would answer. I could hear whispers all around me. I yelled for the people to show themselves but they wouldn't. I collapsed into the snow, sobbing. I felt so alone, cold and vulnerable.

A feeling of safety and security came over me. I was lifted from the cold snow and wrapped in a veil of comfort. I let myself sink deeper into the dream, and blackness came and took over.

When I awoke the next morning I realized there were several more layers of blankets on top of me. I also realized I was in the bed again. I was plastered tightly against Justin's chest. His arms clutched me to him. I started to sit up and the entire world moved and whirled around me.

"Stay lying down," he whispered, stroking my hair.

"Why am I in the bed?" I asked. My voice cracked and my throat felt raw.

"You had a night terror and when I tried to wake you up I realized you were on fire. You've been in and out of it all night. I think the excessive cold just got to you." He twisted my hair around his fingers, playing with it.

"I'm sorry. I'll get up and get ready for work." I tried to shift again but didn't get far.

"No, you'll stay here today and sleep. You're ahead of schedule with your cases, but I can bring some files home with me if you want to look at them this weekend." He shifted to get up.

I noticed he was pale. The circles under his eyes were almost black. "I need to get ready for work."

"I'm sorry," I whispered.

"Don't be. I'm the one that sent you out there in that uniform." He pulled on the first shirt and jeans he found.

"Feel free to use the tablet to surf the web or watch Netflix. You can instant message me if you need anything. Otherwise, stay in bed and get some rest." As if he was on autopilot he bent and pressed a warm kiss to my lips. I froze and so did he.

"I'm sorry," he said, backing away. "Brain... morning... I'm sorry," he said one last time before stepping out the front door.

I blushed as red Santa's suit. I was glad he wasn't there to see it, but I was sure he wasn't much better.

I checked my social media on the tablet then fell asleep again. My dreams were peaceful and warm. I dreamed of that brief kiss and what it would have been like to finish it. I wondered if Justin was demanding like he had to be in daily life or if he was soft and gentle like what he gave me the occasional glimpse of.

Chapter Seven

I heard the click of the door and struggled to sit up. At some point the curtains had been drawn shut and the room was dark. Scared that I really had slept all day I tapped the tablet - it was only noon.

"Justin?"

"Yeah?" I felt the bed dip as he climbed onto it. I wondered if this was a dream or reality.

"Is this real?" I asked.

He laughed and then started to cough. "Yeah, unfortunately. Scoot over." He slid under the blankets next to me.

"Oh no! You caught my cold," I said with a sniffle.

"Yes I did. Now shhhh, let's just get some rest." He wrapped an arm around my waist and pulled me back against him. When he nuzzled the back of my neck a chill ran through me.

"Are you still cold?" he asked, pulling me closer.

I lied. "Yes." He rubbed his hands over me to generate friction. I wasn't ready to admit to him or myself why the chill had really run through my body.

When I awoke I was sprawled halfway across him, our legs in a tangle. I shifted in an attempt to free myself but as I did his grip tightened around me. I stilled as I became increasingly aware of a bulge pressed tightly against my abdomen. As I lay there contemplating its size, a hand reached up and stroked the hair at the nape of my neck and down my back.

"It's alright, I'm here," Justin cooed.

His eyes were closed, his face relaxed with the slightest hint of a grin pulling at his lips. There was the beginning of a dimple showing and his face had just the tiniest bit of stubble. At this moment he was the very definition of handsome. I'm not sure if it was the way he filled my senses with his touch, smell and sight or if it was my fever, but I leaned my head down and pressed my lips to his.

I expected the spell to be broken and for me to withdraw, my kiss a personal secret that he would never remember. Instead his lips parted to mine, and in one motion he tucked me under him and rolled on top of me. His mouth was against mine, demanding but tender. He tasted me, drinking from my lips. I ran my hands over his chest, clinging to him like he was a life preserver.

I gasped when he moved his mouth to my neck and ear. His slight scruff scratched at my sensitive skin and caused me to move against him. His hand expertly slid down to my hip and urged me to wrap a thigh around him. He moved in rhythm, pressing his bulging manhood against me. On a breathless gasp I whispered his name and it caused me to cough.

Instantly he sat up, pulling me into his lap and rubbing my back. From sexual wildcat to nurse in a split second. "I'm sorry Gracie. Are you alright?" he said, his words filled with panic. "I am so sorry, I didn't mean to take advantage of you." When I stopped coughing he slid me onto the bed. "I'll go back to the cot and sleep."

He stood to leave the bed. I quickly lunged for his hand, grasping it with both of mine.

"You didn't do anything wrong. I initiated it." I tugged at him, hoping he would come back to the bed.

"No, it was totally unprofessional of me. Being sick in bed is not initiating it. You have none of the blame. I am in control of my own body-" I tugged him with all my strength, pulling him back down on the bed.

He started to scramble off of it again when I tossed my arms around his shoulders and pressed my lips against his again.

His mouth was hot and at first he resisted. "Like I said, I started it," I mumbled.

He broke the kiss. "Gracie, this goes against all our policies." I shrugged and leaned in to kiss him again. This time I ran my hands over his bare chest. My fingers stopped to play with the small patch of hair there. His mouth opened to me, allowing me to explore it and drink him in. He broke the kiss again.

"You're sick and should get rest. I'm sick and should get some rest as well."

"Shhhh, do you always talk this much? We already have each other's cold." This time he met my kiss full force and fully awake. He reached out and cupped my face in his hands, returning my affection with just as much enthusiasm.

There was a knock at the door. He growled a little but freed himself from my grasp. "Just a moment," he called. He gave me one last apologetic backwards glance as he went to the door. With a tug he opened it. "Hi, Mom."

Joy's voice carried from just outside. "I heard that both you and Gracie were sick. The poor girl has a cold and you came back feeling under the weather yourself. I know how busy you are - I could have taken care of her." There was genuine concern in her voice.

"Mom, there was no point in making more people sick this close to the holidays. I brought work home for both of us this weekend. I am perfectly capable of working and making sure we both eat and get rest." The muscles in his back tensed up as his mother brushed a lock of hair out of his face.

I quietly climbed off the bed and tugged the shirt down so it covered me to mid-thigh. I stepped up beside him with a sniffle. "I'm sorry to have worried you Joy. I think I've just spent too much time outside in too few layers."

Justin wrapped an arm around me, rubbing my shoulder as if the act would keep me warm from the cold outside.

Joy looked me over from head to toe, a slight knowing grin on her lips. "Nonsense, dear. You're so far from home. Having a mother fuss over you a little is a good thing when you're ill. You look dreadfully pale, Gracie, you should stay in and rest for sure. I'll bring the two of you some soup and tea."

"You don't need to make a fuss for my sake. I can come get some dinner when everyone else does," I offered.

"Yeah, Mom don't worry about us. I've just got a little cold. I can come grab stuff and bring it back, worst case scenario. There is no need to trouble yourself."

Joy smiled warmly at both of us, her gaze lingering on her son's arm around my shoulder. She bit back a laugh when he realized he was caught and tried to drop his arm without being seen.

"Oh, I think the two of you should stay in and rest tonight. I'll be back in an hour with some food. Do you have enough wood for the fireplace?"

"Yes, I brought some in this afternoon when I came back. We have plenty." Justin gave his mother a warning look. "Not a word, Mom." She looked surprised. "What are you saying, sweetheart? I just stopped by to make sure my little boy and our guest were alright." She blinked innocently at him.

"Right," he said, rolling his eyes. He pulled me back inside, closing the door behind him.

"What was all that about?" I couldn't help but ask.

"If you give the woman an inch, everyone here will think we are shacked up together and getting married by Christmas."

He sighed heavily and went to sit by the fire. He tugged me onto his lap and pulled a blanket over us both. "What am I going to do with you?"

"I'm not sure what you mean," I told him.

"You showed up sound asleep in the workshop. Even when you first woke up you looked adorable. All I have wanted to do since you arrived was touch you and hold you." He paused. "Don't get me wrong, you're as infuriating as they come."

"All you've wanted to do is hold me and touch me? That sounds a little stalkerish." I shoved away from his chest to look him in the eye. "I am a grown adult woman. It's not appropriate to say things like that. You're not a caveman. I am not a body to be possessed!"

"I know. I fully agree with you. We should keep this professional." He stood up, almost dumping me on the ground. "You have a seat, I'm going to go take a cold shower."

I stumbled but caught hold of his hand. "I didn't say I didn't want to be held and touched."

"Still, you're only here for a short time. We shouldn't get involved. The holidays will come and go, and then you'll be gone."

He smiled. "I'll be back in a bit." I let go of his hand and watched him leave the room. I wandered back to the bed in search of the tablet.

Social media showed pictures of my friends picking out Christmas trees and decorating their houses. It talked about the madness of holiday shopping. I felt a twinge of guilt. My mother loved the holidays and normally I was just as excited, but this year seemed lackluster. I checked my email to find a message from mom as just like I expected.

I smiled as she told me about the happenings at home. She and Dad went and bought a tree. It was too big to fit on top of their new hybrid so they had to have it delivered. The brothers were coming by this weekend to help decorate. Dad recommended that I bake everyone cookies so I could make new friends, and that maybe I could make this a permanent position. I was also reminded that I needed to go get my cell phone and wallet, as my parents had tried calling a number of times.

A knock on the door startled me. "Come in," I called, rolling over to get off the bed. Joy pushed the door open and looked around the room. Her brow furrowed when she noticed her son missing.

"Where is Justin?" she asked while setting a tray of food on the table.

"Taking a shower I believe." I set the tablet down and went to the table. "The food smells divine, Joy, thank you so much. If Justin had known it would be less than an hour I'm sure he wouldn't have gone to shower."

Joy looked at the tablet. "Well, you kids looked hungry. What were you doing on the tablet? Talking to your boyfriend?" I saw the sparkle in her eye and knew immediately she was pumping me for information. I have a mom, I knew all too well how this worked. I bit back the urge to laugh.

Clearing my throat I grabbed the tablet and opened my email, handing it to her. "No, just emailing my parents. I came up here so quickly I didn't bring anything, including my laptop or phone. When they couldn't reach me, they worried."

She read through the email and smiled at the cookies comment. "Ah, so you finished talking to your beau already then?"

I did laugh this time. "No, no guy. I stay busy and just haven't met anyone really... well I just haven't met the right one."

"I see," she shrugged, but her eyes sparkled brightly. "You know, Justin isn't seeing anyone either. He's always too busy, too serious and too stubborn to put his old mother at ease and settle down. He's a good lad though. He hides all his kindness and laughter behind a facade he tries to keep up."

"You don't say?" I leaned over and took a bite of the soup. "Seriously, this is awesome. You make better chicken noodle than my mom... just don't tell her I said that."

Joy chuckled. "Your secret is safe. Since you're staying here, can you do me a favor?" Her voice was sickeningly sweet.

"Sure," I mumbled through the chewing.

"Justin doesn't really decorate for the holidays anymore. Could you do something with the room? I feel dreadful we haven't started decorating the house yet." I blinked at her. My mind raced with how very decorated the house already was.

"Umm, Joy? What do you call the massive tree in the great room? Or all the other stuff around the house?" I was trying to figure out how to address the issue when the door clicked open behind us.

Justin stepped into the room, his hair falling in long sandy brown ringlets. I shook my head. "Wait, wasn't your hair bright red twenty minutes ago?"

He ran his hand through his hair. "Yeah, it was. A few of the guys and I always dye it some bright color for the kickoff of the Holiday season. It washes out really easily though." *Well well well. Tightly wound Justin dyes his hair.*

"Yes, it was blue last year," Joy commented.

"I didn't think I was in there that long," he said, looking at me shoveling food in my mouth.

I swallowed and took a sip of tea. "You weren't, Joy was just very fast," I smiled.

"Well, I should get going. Thanks for your help with the decorations, Grace." Joy made haste to leave the room before I could push the issue.

"She roped you into helping decorate, didn't she?" He shook his head. "I suppose she wants you to decorate in here too, right?"

I nodded.

"That's typical."

"You seem like you're in a better mood," I said without thinking.

"I was in a perfectly fine mood when I left. Sexually frustrated, but just fine." He sat on the ottoman beside me and began to eat.

I eyed him for a moment before taking another bite. "You didn't have to be sexually frustrated."

He choked on his soup. For a split second I was rather pleased with myself until I saw the glare he leveled at me.

"I am your superior. I shouldn't take advantage of you. It's already bad enough you're stuck with me as a roommate. I'm sure you would be much happier with a woman who doesn't snore as much."

"You do know I'm half Werewolf, right? Most of my female cousins snore as loud as or louder than you. Your snoring is downright dainty by comparison," I teased.

"Is that so? Well most of mine don't talk in their sleep nearly as much as you do." He stuck out his tongue at me.

"Because that was mature," I spit back with a smile, baring my teeth.

"On a more serious note, how are you feeling?" His voice changed tone, becoming almost silky with concern.

"Better. Not good, but better. I can walk around without being dizzy, so that's a good start." I pushed the food away. He looked at it with a raised brow. I had only eaten about a third. I was hungry just a few moments ago but now I was just tired. "I think I'm tired."

"Go back to sleep then. I'll take the cot, you can have the bed." I started to argue with him, guilt plaguing me for displacing him. I climbed in the bed and tugged the covers over myself.

"I won't be able to sleep knowing I displaced you onto that cot. I promise to stay on my side of the bed if you'll sleep in it. It's huge, we could fit six of us in it." I patted the space beside me.

"Go to sleep. Maybe by then I'll be tired enough to stay on my own side." I turned over to close my eyes but couldn't fall asleep despite being sleepy. The lights were turned off and I heard the crunch of the cot.

With a heavy sigh I rolled over and crawled to the edge of the bed and off the end of it. I tugged an extra blanket with me and went over beside the cot. I tossed the blanket over the top and Justin raised his head to look up at me. "Thank you," he said sleepily.

"Don't thank me yet." I reached down, tossed back the edge of the blankets and slid onto the cot beside him, pressing my back against his chest, then tugging the covers back up.

He froze all movement including his breathing. "What are you doing?"

"I told you, I can't sleep knowing I took your bed and you're sleeping on the cot. So we can both sleep on the bed like adults, or we can both behave like children and sleep on the cot." I paused, biting my lip. "Or you can sleep on the bed and I will stay on the cot if you are worried I'll get too frisky in my sleep."

He relaxed against me, wrapping an arm around my waist and pulling me tighter against him. I squirmed for a moment until I realized he had again become quite firm and pressed against my backside. "I am not concerned about you getting too frisky. I am concerned about my own actions."

I rolled over in his grip, pressing my curves against him, leaving only inches between our lips. "Obviously, you're attracted to me. I can feel just how much you are." I wiggled my hips against his, causing him to suck in a deep breath. "If I feel the same way, why are you set against it?"

"Because you deserve better than a fling. Don't get me wrong, I love bedsport as much as the next man, but there are women you know that if you indulge in, you'll want more." He shrugged.

"I'm here for almost three more weeks. There can be more." I leaned forward and kissed him. His body responded to mine.

He pulled back with a shaky breath. "I don't mean more time in bed. I mean more, as in relationship more. I would want more than you can give," he finished. "I've had Holiday flings and it always ends the same. She goes home and I stay here alone. Forgive me for saying this, but I don't want that with you."

It certainly had the desired effect. My jets cooled and I leaned my head against his shoulder. I thought about what he was saying and considered it carefully. The last thing I wanted to do was rush into a relationship, but there was an obvious spark between us. "Woo me."

"What?" The confusion was thick in his voice.

"Woo me. You know, take me out on dates. Let's see if there is something there beyond sexy sparks." I smiled at him with my best thousand-watt grin.

He eyed me carefully. "And what do you think is going to happen? I've dated before and I'm still available. Has it occurred to you that I'm a workaholic and bad at relationships? That's why I'm single."

"Has it occurred to you maybe you just haven't found the right person? You live in a place that is all about magic, why don't you believe there is any of it out there for you?" I wiggled free of his grip and climbed off the cot, giving him my best come-hither look.

"You think you're the right girl?" Amusement laced through his words.

"That's the thing, you'll never know if you don't try. I could be a big mistake or I could be the best thing ever. All I know is that I'm going to get in this bed. You can come over here and sleep if you want. You can come over here and find out if I'm any good at this bedsport thing you are talking about. OR you can stay there and never know. Up to you, boss man. Just know I may get very cold tonight without you to keep me warm." With that I slid back under the covers on the bed.

The room was silent for a long time but then I head the creak of the cot. When I didn't hear him move after that I thought maybe he had just rolled over. Without warning he slid under the covers beside me and pulled me against his chest. "I wouldn't be able to live with myself if you got cold and ended up even sicker than you are now." I smiled as his warmth radiated into me.

His hand slid to my hip and under the edge of the shirt I wore. He lightly traced circles over my stomach with his fingertips. It tickled and at the same time was arousing. When his hand came to rest on my breast, I sucked in a shaky breath. It rested there for a moment, unmoving and tormenting in its stillness. Then his thumb brushed over my peak, sending tingling shocks all through me. When he did it again I felt it tighten under his touch and a quiet moan escaped me.

"Oh, I think I like that," he whispered in my ear, before doing it again.

With the next moan he urged me to turn over so he could unbutton the shirt. His fingers made fast work of the buttons and before I had time to react I was once again exposed to him. He lowered his head and ran his tongue along the valley between my breasts, cupping one in his hand, slowly caressing it with intensity. When he brought his mouth to the other, taking its hardened tip between his lips and teasing it lightly with his teeth, my body jerked under his touch, causing me to moan again - but this time filled with need.

He chuckled, lifting his mouth to capture mine. The kiss almost tickled because of his amusement. I traced the lines of his chest and abs with my hands as the kiss deepened. My hands ran lower until I realized he had also shed his clothes before coming to bed. I wrapped my hand around him, causing him to bite my lip in surprise.

Cautiously at first I stroked him. He allowed his head to lull back and narrowed his eyes. As I sped up my pace, his breathing caught as he reached down and captured my wrist. I started to pout at the prospect of having my new toy taken away so soon.

"I am still not at one hundred percent. I suggest if you want me to show you anything remotely impressive about my bedsport capabilities you stop now, or else I may fall short of your expectations." I released him and let my hands make their way back up his chest. I ran my fingers through the soft patch of hair there.

"Just enough to be manly without being too much," I chimed in.

He caressed my hips and urged my thighs to part for him. Tracing imaginary patterns on my inner thighs he parted me further until his hand rested against my mound. He leaned down and captured my mouth as he caressed the folds and lips of my most intimate parts. I gasped as he pressed a finger to my core, instinctively thrusting my hips at him and tightening my muscles around him.

He started slowly caressing my delicate pearl with the same motions his tongue made on mine. I moaned and twisted under him, urging him to go fast, but he continued slowly, causing a fire to ignite low in my loins. With each intimate touch and caress I felt the fire grow hotter and bigger within me. Each time I would get close to being pushed over the edge he would stop or change his technique just a little. Finally my body won out and I tumbled over in a moment of white-hot ecstasy.

"There, how does that feel?" he cooed in my ear. I nodded my happy approval, my thighs quivering.

He then moved between my thighs, kneeling there. He urged me to open wider and wrap my legs around his hips. I felt the tip of his manhood press against my opening and I moaned as if he had already entered. With one hard thrust he buried himself deep within me. He was thicker and longer than I had ever experienced and my whole body screamed happily as it adjusted to accommodate him.

When he withdrew I cried out in protest, until he thrust deep into me again. This time though, he set to work with a fast and hard rhythm. I ran one hand down his back while I pulled him down to kiss me with the other. He turned his head and pressed his mouth to my neck, sending chills down my spine.

"I want to hear you," he whispered by my ear, and to prove his point took extra care with the next thrust.

Soon I was gasping for air, unable to think. All I could do was hold on. He was pushing me higher than I had ever gone, causing me to make noises I didn't know I could, and then I teetered on the edge of something great and with his next thrust all was lost. I crashed over the cliff screaming out his name and begging him never to let go. I felt myself tightening around him, causing him to thrust harder to keep pace and then the sound of my climax and reactions pushed him over the edge. He cried out his own release, burying himself deeply within me one last time.

We lay there panting, covered in a thin veil of sweat in each other's arms. He moved and pressed a kiss to my lips. It was deep, passionate and spoke of promises yet to come. "Let's get some sleep, because tomorrow I start trying to 'woo' you." I giggled before I drifted off in his arms.

Chapter Eight

The next morning I awoke to the sound of dishes clinking together. I lifted my head and peered in the direction of the noise. Justin shifted under me, running a hand down my back. There was a shadow by the fireplace and the only other person who should be in the room was plastered against me. "Hello?" I whispered to the darkness.

Joy's voice answered back, "Oh sorry, I didn't mean to wake you. Go back to sleep."

For the first time in my life, in the dark of the room, modesty hit me and I tugged blankets up over my head. I cringed inwardly at the thought of being caught in bed with someone's son. I heard the door click open and closed and saw the soft glow of sunlight through the blanket. I lowered my head back to Justin's chest trying not to focus on how I could die of embarrassment.

"Good morning," chirped a happy male voice. Hands ran down the curve of my back, cupping my rump. In a fluid motion Justin tossed back the covers

and rolled over, pinning me beneath him. He dipped
his head and caught my mouth with his in a sweet
soft kiss that was over way too quickly. Leaning back
he brushed the hair from my face. "How are you
feeling this morning?"

"Mortified!" My skin still was pink with blush.

"Oh," he said, and started to roll off of me. I
grabbed his shoulders and went with him, pinning
him back on the bed and straddling his hips.

"Your mother was in here this morning. I think she
came in for the dishes. Did you think I was mortified
about us? And last night?" Before he could answer I
leaned down and ran my tongue over his neck and
nipped his earlobe. I explained in a voice that was
still garbled by sleep, "I was embarrassed at being
caught naked in the arms of a man by his mother. It
had nothing to do with being in *your* arms."

He chuckled, causing his whole body to vibrate,
including the bulge pressed against me where I
straddled him. "That's why I always return my
dishes, because she will just come in. It made the teen
years difficult." I laughed. He ran a hand along my
thigh and allowed it to rest on my hip. His other felt
around the headboard until I heard a click. The

curtains along the large window opened and sunlight spilled into the room.

He looked down along the length of his body to where I sat spread across him. I felt his bulge throb under me and almost whimpered. The prior night had been amazing. His eyes continued to drift up, lingering a moment on my breasts before meeting my eyes. "You're beautiful first thing in the morning. Do you know that?" I felt my blush return.

"So what is the plan for the day? Starting today you were going to try and woo me, remember?" I laughed. I started to try and move off of him but his hands came firmly to my hips and held me in place.

"I could just keep you in bed all day and try to impress you more with my prowess in the sheets." I smiled imagining that.

Finally I shook my head. "I want to see your home. Have you lived here your whole life?"

The smile on his face radiated so brightly it was almost blinding. The dimple in his left cheek showed and for a moment I was mesmerized. "Yes, I have lived here my whole life. All two hundred and nineteen years of it."

"Have you ever left the North Pole?" I asked. "To visit other places?"

"Of course, but not nearly as often since I accepted the position overseeing operations when my father retired. Honestly, I always thought one of my sisters would take the position. My sister Helen and I were the only two that stuck around to help with the family business. My other sisters do come every year and work during the Holidays, but they had no desire to stay at the Pole."

"Well, I want to see everything." I successfully slid off of him this time. "But first I want to go eat breakfast." He must have been in full agreement because at the mention of breakfast he was out of bed and dressing quickly as well.

About ten minutes later we wandered into the large dining room of the main house. The seats were packed wall to wall. There must have been nearly forty people. When we finally stumbled in, Justin's arm affectionately around my waist, the room that had been loud and lively with noise came to a complete halt. The silence was deafening.

Finally Joy broke the ice. "How are the two of you feeling today?"

"Much better, thank you. I still have a tickle in my throat, but the fever is gone." I smiled awkwardly. The break in silence seemed to be all that was needed to send the crowd back to their discussions. Justin let go of my waist and snagged my wrist instead, leading me through the crowd to sit by Joy.

"Grace, you've already met my mother." He motioned to two men seated beside her. One had grey hair and a long mustache with braids in it. The other had long white hair and a long white beard, also adorned with a few scattered braids. "This is my father Lucus, and this is my uncle Markus, he's the current..."

"Santa Claus!" I smiled.

"Yeah," finished Justin with an eye roll.

I beamed brightly at Lucus and Markus. One look at the two of them and there was no doubt they were brothers. Lucus took my hand and gave it an affectionate squeeze while Markus just gave me a wink.

"I've heard you've been a very good girl this year," said Markus.

Both Justin and I choked. "Stopping a war, bringing me back some of the royal brew, protecting baby Dragons, saving villages, and all while not complaining about the fashion disaster we dressed you in." We exchanged looks and relaxed a little. "Why, you've even gotten our favorite grumpy control freak to lighten up."

"Grumpy control freak?" The question just tumbled out. "Who?"

"He means Justin, dear," said Joy, adding pancakes to my plate while I was distracted.

"Justin is a grumpy control freak?" I looked at his family then back at Justin. I laughed before readdressing Santa. "I think you're being a little too hard on him. He's just doing his job but he's not like that when he's not working." Everyone around me exchanged looks. "He's not," I insisted.

Justin beamed with pride - as if I had just won the third grade spelling bee. I had given an honest answer, but evidentially he and I were the only ones who thought it was true. He patted my leg affectionately then pointed to the plate in front of me. "Eat up, we have a busy day." I didn't need to be told twice and dug into the plate before me.

Soon I had my face pressed tightly against Justin's back as I clung to him for dear life. The chill of icy cold air whipped by as our snowmobile cut through the snow-covered hills. We swung around a tight corner and I had to resist the urge to scream. When we slid to a stop I stumbled off, crashing to my knees. I was so glad to be on solid ground.

"Are you alright?" asked a tall Dark Elf. He held out a hand to help me up.

Taking his hand I was hauled to my feet. "Thank you." Justin appeared just as I managed to get my feet back under me. He wrapped an arm around my waist giving me extra support. I brushed the stray hair from my face and smiled at the owner of the hand I now held. "Hi there, I'm Grace MacGregor, Holiday Spirit."

"I'm Marthailain Darinuss. Are you any relation to Ian MacGregor?" He gave my hand a quick pump before letting it go.

"Actually, yes. He's my cousin and the future Chieftain of my clan. Are you a friend of his?" Curiosity was getting the better of me. Perhaps this man knew more about the mysterious girlfriend.

"I am the current Elder overseeing Asia for the OAC. He's involved with two young women under my guardianship there." He paused, sensing my apprehension. "Maybe 'involved with' isn't the right term. He's dating one and friends with the other." He nodded, confirming his word choice.

I laughed. "No worries. His new girlfriend is a bit of a mystery for the family. Can you tell me anything about her?" I asked nonchalantly.

"Ah, well, Alizeyah is a bit of a rarity. She's a Halfling Dragon and Elven Tempest who was left as a Changeling in the Human realm. She can be a bit of a handful, but she's a sweet young woman when she keeps her mouth shut." He grinned, obviously recalling some moment that cemented his description. "She tempers Ian's occasional gloominess and he keeps her grounded. I think they're a good match."

Part of me breathed a sigh of relief. It sounded like she was at least approachable, which would make my upcoming case easier. "Well that makes me feel better. I'm sure my parents will breathe a little easier knowing he's in good hands."

"Indeed." Marthailain turned his attention to Justin. "Good to see you again, sir. Is this your new Lady?"

Justin sucked in a breath, obviously uncomfortable with assigning a title. "She's a close friend. Up here to get a tree?"

The Dark Elf nodded slowly. "As you know, Birda is passionate about Christmas and Yule. It's in her contract that I will get her a tree to decorate each year. Since Seoul doesn't allow the sale of live cut Christmas trees I have to bring it in with magic. I keep hoping each year she will let me buy her a fake one."

Justin laughed. "Gnomes can be a little intense. I don't see her agreeing to a fake tree anytime soon. Besides, you know we have the best cold stout up here. Make sure you stop by and buy a keg or two to take back with you. This year's is particularly nice." He and Marthailain shook hands and we parted ways.

"So are we up here to get a tree?" I asked as I leaned into him while we walked.

"We are, along with a wreath and some garlands. Mom wants the room decorated, so we're going to decorate it." His eyes twinkled.

"Can I drive back?" I smiled, hoping he would agree. Then I could take it a little slower over all the hills.

"We'll see. I can't say I would object to wrapping myself around you." There was a youthful, carefree spirit to him today. We wandered through the forest of trees discussing the pros and cons of each tree.

"I see how it is," he said abruptly.

"You see how what is?" I was stumped.

"You're a size queen. You keep writing off the short ones, but sometimes when they are all dressed up they look the best." His grin was purely wicked.

"I do like the tall ones, but it's really about the branches for me. How much can they hold? Are they full or lacking?" I laughed.

"Are we talking about the same thing? I was making an innuendo and at first I thought you were too. Now, I think you may be actually talking about trees," he teased.

I shrugged. "Maybe I am."

"Maybe you are what?" His eyes narrowed on me. "You're intentionally being a pain." His laugh was deep and I felt the smallest twinge of something in my chest. "You know, I'm in good with Santa. You keep it up and I can make sure you're on the Naughty list forever."

I walked over to him, wrapped my arms around his neck, and kissed him. I pressed myself tightly against him. He embraced me and returned the kiss. When I finally broke it, I gave him a wink. "You may like me naughty."

"I *really* like naughty." He grinned widely. It was then I realized he had two dimples. He had a matching set. "What? Your face just took on a glow of pure joy."

"You have two dimples!" I poked each of them with my gloved fingers. He reached up and took both my hands in his.

"I do, but it's a secret. If you tell anyone, I'll have to kill you." His dimples never disappeared.

"I bet that gets you on the naughty list for a really long time."

He kissed my nose and turned back to look at the tree. "So what do you think? This one?"

I walked around it one last time before agreeing. "This will work. Now where do we go for the garland? All that has to be hand strung, right?"

"We are entrepreneurs here. People come from all the realms to buy top grade North Pole products each year. There is a shop that sells greenery not far from here." He pulled out a saw from the bag he had over his shoulder. "Let's get this guy cut down."

Soon we had the tree wrapped in a tarp and tied behind the snowmobile. Justin climbed behind me and pulled me back into the curve of his thighs. I relaxed into him. We glided along the surface of the snow towards a small shop close to the main house. When we pulled up Justin helped me off and then checked the ropes on the tree and tarp. "Go ahead inside and get warm, I'll be in shortly."

The shop was cozy and reminded me of roadside stops in Vermont and New Hampshire. The walls were lined with green garlands and wreaths, some already adorned with bows and flowers. I began gathering armfuls of the greenery. I was turning to head to the register when a strong pair of arms swooped in and relieved me of my burden. "Are we decorating the room or the whole house?" Justin teased.

"Just the room, but I need a few more things." I quickly piled two more wreaths, a couple boxes of lights, some electronic candles and a roll of red ribbon on top of the pile.

Stumbling to the register Justin handed the bounty to the cashier to sort out. "How are you paying for all this, Lady?" He smiled at me.

"Oh, you get to pay for it. It's your room, I'm just the help. Besides, when you zapped me up here it was without my phone, purse, or wallet."

He rolled his eyes. "Do I look like your sugar Dwarf?" he asked.

"No, but you look like a man attempting to woo me and make his mother happy as well." I poked him in the shoulder.

"Ah, playing the mom card. That's a low blow to any man. I guess I have no choice." He pulled out his wallet and handed the cashier a credit card.

"You take plastic up here?"

"Of course, we accept Visa, Master Card and recently Amex. We also have a credit union." He signed the slip of paper and thanked the girl attempting to wrestle the greenery into bags. "You're going to have to drive home slowly since I'll only be able to hold on with one arm. Someone decided to buy too much stuff." His teasing made me blush as I noticed the people both working and shopping had taken notice of us.

When we got outside I poked at him a bit. "So why does everyone stare at us?"

"Probably because they are wondering how I managed to snag the prettiest girl up North." I laughed as he shrugged. "It's been several years since anyone has seen me decorate or with a girl that I wasn't related to."

"That sounded kind of kinky in a bad way," I commented as I climbed on the snowmobile.

"Yeah it did, but you get what I mean. I just don't date. It never ends well. Girls here are either here for a month or two and then leave or they've been here their entire lives and I already know them. It gets harder each time you make a connection with someone and she leaves. You stay in touch for a little bit, but by the following year she has a new guy." He wrapped his arm tightly around my waist as we began the journey back to the house.

"So why get attached." I nodded my head in understanding. "Have you ever considered leaving the Pole?"

"Sure, but this is in my blood. Would you give up being a Werewolf if it meant you could have a normal life with a Human? If it was the only way you could be with them?" he asked.

"It's in my blood. I can't give it up. If they were the right person for me, my wolf blood wouldn't matter." I understood what he was saying. The North Pole was as much part of his blood as my Were half. "Do you think it's selfish expecting a girl to give up her life to be here?"

I felt him shrug. "Maybe it is. Who knows, maybe I could give it all up to be with the right girl, but when people are only here for a month or two at most it's hard to know if it's a forever sort of connection."

I chewed my lip the rest of the way back to the house. I wasn't sure what to say. I understood why he didn't want to get involved with me or anyone, but I couldn't help but feel like this was involved and not just a fling. We pulled up alongside the house so we wouldn't have to haul the tree any further than needed. "This should be good," he said in my ear as I cut the engine.

He handed me the bag of greenery and nodded towards the door. "Can you take this in and I'll wrestle the tree?" I saluted him and took the bag, pushing the door open. I dropped the bag on the table and went back to help him anyway. He didn't need me. He picked up the tree like it was nothing and brought it in, practically tripping over me where I stood in the door way. "Oops, sorry. Are you alright?"

"Yeah, no harm no foul," I said as I cleared out of the way.

Justin kicked the door shut and leaned the tree against the wall. He went to the closet to rummage around and when he pulled out four large boxes I was flabbergasted as to where they had come from. He also pulled out a tree stand and slid it across the floor. "This is what I have for decorations. There are more in the main house if we need them."

"You have four boxes for one room?" I teased.

"Yeah, it's sort of sparse I know, but I stopped decorating a number of years ago." He straightened up and rolled his shoulders back.

"That wasn't a commentary on how few you had but rather the opposite - I have three boxes for my entire apartment and one of those is my fake tree." I knelt by the fireplace to add logs so we could start a new blaze.

"You have a fake tree? I knew you were too good to be true. I can't see you anymore." He knelt beside me and helped arrange the logs, then lit them.

"I like live trees, but living alone in a tiny apartment on the other side of the country doesn't lend itself to live trees much. I have a small potted tree I decorate every year. Does that count?" I took his hand when he offered it to help me stand back up.

He rubbed his chin. "I guess I can make an exception. Since I'm a bachelor I understand what it's like to have time constraints."

"You're so considerate," I teased.

It took us the better part of the afternoon, but soon the room looked like something out of a magazine. Its rustic charm was enhanced with garlands around the door, hearth, headboard, and window. I used ribbon to hang three wreaths along the window and one on the door. The mantle of the fireplace displayed a collection of a dozen nutcrackers, each handmade. His family photos were mixed between them. The room and tree sparkled with twinkling white lights and glass ornaments. All that was missing was a star atop the tree. "Do you have a tree topper?" I asked, looking around the room.

"Actually, no. I can go get one though," he offered.

"I have a better idea, if you're up for a little magical travel. I would like to go home to grab my electronics, my purse, and maybe some undergarments, and we can grab my Holiday decorations. I have a beautiful glass star that would look awesome," I smiled.

"You know, it's against the rules for you to leave the North Pole until your contract is over." He considered me. "Make me a list and tell me where to find things and I'll go get them for you."

I hadn't thought of the possibility of him going without me. "What should I do while you're gone?" I thought maybe I could get him to bend the rules.

"Oh, I have an idea." He handed me a pen and a pad of paper. "You make that list and I'll be right back." I quickly scribbled a list on the paper and did my best to remember where things were. When he reappeared a few moments later it was with a sprig of mistletoe in hand.

Dangling the mistletoe overhead he leaned down to kiss me. I wanted to be serious but I couldn't stop smiling. "Testing it to make sure it's not defective before you hang it up?"

"Actually I just wanted to do that, but that's a great cover story." Justin reached up and hung it on an exposed beam overhead. "Is your list ready?" I nodded, handing it to him. He read over it quickly. "Ok, I'll be back shortly. Oh, and I'm really sorry for what's about to happen."

Before I could ask what that was, he was gone in a swirl of sparkling snow and there was a knock on the door. "Coming," I called. When I opened the door Joy was there with an apron in hand. "Cookie baking?" She nodded with a smile.

Chapter Nine

I was sitting with my feet on the ottoman, stretched out in front of the fireplace, when the air swirled again with glittering fake snow. I popped another cookie in my mouth as I watched the overloaded Justin appear. He had my large rolling luggage, two boxes of decorations, my computer bag, purse and ice skates. "Your apartment is cute. A little cluttered - I've never seen so many shoes in a closet before."

I laughed. "You were gone a long time. I made three types of cookies." I held out the plate as an offering. He considered options before popping a sugar cookie in his mouth.

"I took my time while choosing extra clothes for you. I thought you may need some other warm stuff." He sat everything down and opened the suitcase. Half of it was lingerie.

"How are corsets and garter belts going to keep me warmer?" I laughed.

"Easy! If you wear them, I will keep you warm. Problem solved." Both his dimples were back with full force.

I moved the clothes to the closet. "Is there a reason you packed a cocktail dress for me?" I asked as I pulled my black glittery dress from the suitcase.

"There is a big party Christmas Eve; we give Santa a sendoff and then enjoy the fruits of our labors." He paused. "If you want to stay. Your contract will be over so you could go home to your parents." The dimples faded.

He added familiar pictures to the mantle above the fire - photos of my family and friends. It was a thoughtful touch that made the place feel more like home for me. Together we unpacked and hung the decorations. When the time came for the star I began to move the ottoman but he swept me into his arms and lifted me the extra foot or so I needed.

"It's perfect." I smiled. I looked around the room, admiring our handiwork. "I have an idea." Grabbing his tablet I tugged him in front of the tree. "We need a selfie!" We snapped a dozen pictures of ourselves around the room.

Joy knocked on the door. "Are you two coming to dinner?" she asked, pushing open the door. She froze, looking around the room. Her eyes welled up with tears. "It's beautiful! You haven't decorated in years." She considered her son for a moment then pushed him aside, giving me a big hug. "Thank you!" she whispered into my ear.

"You're welcome. I didn't really do anything though." I hugged her back, realizing how much I missed my own mother.

"You've done more than you could ever understand." She whirled around to face Justin. She kissed him on the cheek and whispered something in his ear. His eyes flared with surprise.

At dinner the table was abuzz with talk and laughter. More people arrived with each meal. Dinner was a selection of winter veggies, fresh bread and ribs. What was left of the brew I brought back from the Dwarven Stronghold was passed around the table, causing conversations to run more freely. At least a half-dozen members of the family asked us when our binding ceremony was. I'm not sure who stuttered more, Justin or me.

I offered to help clean up, but the aunts and cousins refused, all but pushing me out the door. All things considered I did want to take a look at the cases that Justin had brought back Friday. If I could get a jump start on them before Monday I would feel better prepared. I slipped away back to his room.

I sat facing the fire with my laptop in front of me. There was an email that had come from the company that bought out Bob's business. They wanted to know if I was available for an interview. I considered what to say and ultimately decided to see if they would do a video call interview. Leaving the North Pole wasn't an option until after my contract was up.

I closed the laptop and reached for the files. They were Ian's and the lady who didn't want her assistant to leave. The first one seemed easy enough. I was still confused on the second one. I needed to find a way that everyone could win. The way I saw it either the assistant or the old woman was going to lose out.

I looked at the clock. It was roughly seven in the morning in Seoul. I grabbed my phone from where it had been charging. Flipping through the numbers I found Ian's cell and hit call. On the third ring there was a click followed by a gruff voice. "Grace, what's wrong?"

"I spoke with Marthailain today - I really need to speak with Alizeyah. It's an emergency." I did my best to sound official.

"Why do you need to speak with Kat?" he asked, concern seeping into his speech.

"I thought her name was Alizeyah?" The question just slipped out.

"It is. That's her actual name. Her Human name is Kathryn," he corrected. I heard him speaking in muffled tones.

"Hello?" There was a voice on the other end that sounded confused and innocent. She sounded like she was ten years old.

"Hello Kat, my name is Grace and I'm Ian's cousin. I need you to pay close attention and only answer yes or no to my questions. Do you understand?" I grimaced a little, feeling bad to be worrying Ian like this.

"Yes."

"Has Ian asked you about coming to meet the family this Yule and Christmas?"

"No."

"Ok, give him a few days and if he doesn't bring it up, you ask him. You must go to Boston with him. It's very important that you do this. Can you do that?" I drilled the question.

"Ummmmm..."

"That wasn't a yes or no. Ian doesn't know this, but it's a really big deal he's there and he is going to need your love and support through the holidays. Do you understand?" I prodded her again.

"Yes."

"Can I count on you to get him there and be with him? You can bring friends if you want to."

"Alright, I'll take care of it." She sounded more awake now.

"Excellent. Thank you for helping out. I wouldn't ask if it wasn't important," I told her before hanging up the phone. I needed to email Mom and let her to know to expect two to four more. I filled out the completion paperwork that went with the case and slid it into the folder.

The door clicked open. "Gracie, are you in here?" Justin said as he opened the door to find me working. His face softened. "Workaholic," he accused.

"Why hello there, Mr. Kettle, and how are you feeling today?"

"Very fine and black, Ms. Pot, and yourself?"

"Just as pitch as coal, thank you for asking!" I couldn't help but laugh. Justin rolled his eyes.

"Since I didn't work yesterday I wanted to make sure I wasn't falling behind. I want to get my ten contractual cases taken care of." I reached out to take his hand, giving it an affectionate squeeze.

His face fell. "Do you want out of here that bad?"

"No, nothing like that. There is a huge backlog of cases that are years old. If I finish early I figured I could address some of those. Clean out ones that no longer need addressed. Your Holiday Spirit department is a disaster." He considered my words for a long moment before letting some of the worry leave his face.

"Maybe you should slow down with your cases. I don't want you to burn out." He sat on the ottoman beside me.

"I just finished my fifth case," I told him, closing the folder.

"Just like that, while I was helping clear the table?" There was disbelief in his voice.

"Yep. Halfway done," I answered with a confident grin.

He took the folders and laptop from my lap and placed them on the table. Then in a movement out of a movie he swept me up out of the chair and cradled me in his arms. "I'm glad you're so productive. I don't have to feel bad about taking you to bed and keeping you there all day tomorrow."

"Why would you feel bad about that?" I smiled what I hoped was a seductive grin. "I like the sound of that plan."

"Because you may be very sore tomorrow after what I have planned tonight" he gave me a wink.

"I've never been all that kinky... but what the heck. I'll try anything once." I leaned against him. "Should I tie you down and lick every inch of you?"

His breath caught in his throat. "Not quite what I had in mind but we will absolutely add that to the agenda for tomorrow." He pulled a scarf out of his pocket.

"Oh a blindfold, that could be fun too."

He chuckled. "Yes it could." He reached out and tied it over my eyes. "Do you trust me?"

"Of course", I said and the scary thing was... it was true. Totally true.

"Good."

I didn't struggle when he helped me into a coat and boots although I had pictured clothing coming off and not going on. He took my hand and led me out into the cold night air.

"Are you sure we should be out here while we are recovering from colds?"

"Probably not, but there is something I want to show you." He continued to guide me through the snow for a walk that seemed to last forever.

"Ok, sit down." His voice was tentative but warm. He guided me to sit. I reached up to take off the blindfold but he stopped me.

"Leave it on." I felt him sit beside me and was startled when he reached down and pulled my boots off. Just as quickly he slid me feet into the familiar fit of my ice skates.

"Lace the right one first, tight over the instep and room through the ankle." He laughed but followed directions.

"Your control freak is showing," he teased.

"I spent a lot of years skating. I have a method."

"Were you a figure skater then?" he asked as he smoothed my pants leg down.

"No, but my father loved to take Michael and I skating. We did it almost every weekend as far back as I can remember." I felt the smile creep into my voice and then suddenly his mouth was there kissing that smile.

When he withdrew I felt like something was missing. "That was a beautiful memory. I only hope you remember this with a fraction of the joy you just showed me."

Taking my hands he guided me across the rubbery terrain. When we stopped he picked me up and cradled me against his chest. I felt the glide of ice underneath us. When he sat me down again there was an anticipation between us that was charged and harmonious.

I felt his fingers tug at my blindfold and then it happened. The world was flooded with twinkling lights. We were standing in the middle of a small pond with lights hung on every available branch, fencepost or surface they could be secured to. It was like a million tiny stars reflecting off the surface of the pond.

"Oh, it's the most beautiful thing I think I've ever seen."

He grinned that special smile with two dimples just for me, then took my hand. "Skate with me, Gracie."

We laughed and twirled about the glassy surface of the pond among all the twinkling stars and lights until we were so frozen neither of us could feel our legs or faces anymore. When he tugged me to a stop once more at the center of the ice, it was to capture my face between his freezing hands and lower his lips to mine.

They were warm against mine and I found myself leaning into the kiss. I wanted more and I never wanted it to stop. When he finally broke the kiss he held me against his chest. "I feel like you belong here, held against me like this. Grace, I'm afraid."

I knew exactly what he meant. I felt at home in his arms listening to his heartbeat. Wrapping my arms tighter around him I snuggled as tightly as I could. "What are you afraid of?"

"I'm afraid I'm falling and you might not be there to catch me."

I took a deep breath. "I will be, if you let me," I whispered.

Taking my hand in his he guided me back off the ice. "Let's get back in so I can warm you up. I think I may need to keep you warm all night tonight and all day tomorrow."

"Does that mean more bedsport?" I asked jokingly.

"Of course, can you think of a better way to keep warm?" He tugged at my hand, pulling me against him for another kiss.

"If you keep kissing me we'll freeze to death."

"No we won't. Have you ever made love in the snow?" There was a wicked gleam in his eyes as he asked.

"No, but I think that is better left until we are both fully recovered from our colds." That seemed to be all the encouragement he needed because he was rushing me back towards the house at almost a run.

"What's the rush?" I asked

"I want to warm you up right now." He turned to look at me over his shoulder.

"With all the naughty things you brought back is there anything you would like me to wear?" I was hoping the playful suggestion would add to the moment.

"Yes, I want you to wear the blindfold and only the blindfold." I froze where I stood, thinking about it for a moment. He quickly added, "Only if you want to."

"Oh I do, only if you'll wear it for me too," I purred at him. That's all it took and I was tossed over his shoulder while he sprinted the rest of the way back to the house.

Once in and behind closed doors we only separated long enough to remove our clothing before diving into the warmth of the bed and each other's arms.

Bedsport turned to lovemaking and true to his words, I was barely allowed to leave bed on Sunday. I was allowed a few trips to the bathroom but otherwise we slept, made love, ate, cuddled, watched movies and did it all over again from the comfort of his large rustic bed.

Chapter Ten

Monday came all too quickly but I was going to kick it off with a new uniform. When I walked into Maggie's office I wasn't surprised that I was met with a look of disgust. "I've come for a different uniform."

She gave me a sinister smile. "I'm afraid that's all we have in your size."

"You see, I know for a fact, that's not true. I could go get Justin, but Joy told me to let you know that she would personally come down and help you find one if need be." I forced a big wolfy grin showing lots of teeth.

Maggie rolled her eyes then trotted off out of sight. When she returned a few minutes later she carried more white garments, but these looked heavier. "You still have to wear the wreath. But here is a new gown and a white wool coat."

I looked over the garments and signed the slip. "Are we done here?"

"I hope so. Please don't make me look at you until after Christmas." She started to go back to work and then stopped. "Everyone here is talking about the two of you. Justin is special. He's been hurt too many times. Don't lead him on."

"I'm not leading him on," I told her, but I started asking myself what was going to happen after the Holidays.

Gathering the clothes into my arms I made haste to leave the uniform room and make it to my office on time. When I arrived the room was full of chatter - which died the second I stepped through the doorway. Everyone stared at me with wide eyes. I cleared my throat uncomfortably. "Ummm, good morning. Did everyone have a nice weekend?"

Nobody answered me. They just kept staring. "Ok, well sounds like you all had quiet weekends then. Good for you. I'm just going to log in and get some work done." As I sat at my desk I flipped through the stacks of folders in front of me. I pulled out a couple cases that I thought I could resolve this morning with some phone calls and online detective work. I was just preparing to go find a cup of coffee when Mary plopped in the chair beside me.

"Good morning," she said with a grin.

It was so nice to see a smile I relaxed a little. "It is. Maggie gave me a uniform I won't freeze to death in." I motioned to the clothes covered in plastic garment bags.

"Oh, that *is* a good way to start Monday," she agreed. Mary leaned close, dropping her voice to a whisper. "Everyone is shocked that you spent the weekend with Justin. They want to know if that's how you got out of work Friday. He left early that day."

I had the urge to roll my eyes. "Actually I was caught in a blizzard working on a case with a missing Dragon artifact. I ended up getting a cold. My fever was high enough he insisted I not work Friday. I did still complete a case this weekend though, so it wasn't a total bust."

She shuddered. "I hate working with Dragons - glad it was you and not me. It sounds like you're keeping up with your case load then. How many of your ten do you have done?" She seemed sincerely interested.

"I finished number five Saturday night. I think I may be able to resolve three more by lunch if things go my way." I looked at the files I had set to the side.

Her jaw dropped. "You haven't been here a week and you've almost completed your ten?" Her voice was no longer hushed. Everyone was once again staring at me. "You must really want out of here."

I waved the idea a way. "No, it's not like that. I can see there is a backlog of cases that need done. I figure when I finish my assigned number I can begin working on the backlog." A mumble ran through the small office.

Mary leaned close again. "Are you trying to make us all look bad?"

I laughed. "No, not at all. I just want to do a good job and help out. I have the time. I don't have a job to rush home to, so why not?"

"I'll tell you why not. They used to have a really hard time getting workers for this department. Enough so that it became a paid position, and it's a pretty comfy gig when you think about only needing to complete ten cases. If you make it look too easy they may change it." She glanced around the room again. "If you're seeing the boss and over-performing... are you trying to land a supervisor position?"

"It would seem everyone here is more concerned about what is going on outside of office hours then during. I'm not trying to get a supervisor position, I'm not trying to make people look bad, I just want to do a good job and I like helping people. Is that so wrong?" I felt like beating my head against the desk.

Mary took my hand in hers. "I understand. Let me give you some advice then. Don't get involved with Justin. At the end of the season you'll leave and he'll stay. One or both of you will get hurt. You seem like a nice girl. Listen to me, I have a hundred years of wisdom on you." She smiled before sliding out of the chair and returning to her own desk.

I opened the files again and began working. By lunch I had finished the three files I had pulled out, plus two more. I was officially done with my ten. Everything I did from here on out was bonus. I went to the cafeteria feeling almost weightless. As I stood in line to get a salad a thought struck me. I grabbed a cup of coffee and returned my tray, rushing to get back to my desk.

I opened the browser and checked my email. Sure enough, there was a message from the company that wanted to interview me. They were surprised to know I hadn't returned to the East Coast yet but were happy to do a video call interview. They asked if I was free Tuesday afternoon. After I compared time stamps I set it up for lunch time so all I had to do was find a quiet place. Before closing my email I opened the one from Justin. It had some of our selfies in it. I smiled as I flipped through them, making sure to close it down before everyone returned.

After lunch I pulled on my new dress. It was sleeveless and white with a deep plunging neckline. It seemed very ethereal when I moved in it. The gem, though, was white wool duster trimmed in silver braid with an oversized hood. Maggie had been nice enough to include red fur-trimmed gloves to go with it. I was toasty warm when I departed to check on my case involving the mistreated assistant.

I had been right. The older woman was terribly lonely, but it didn't justify her treating her assistant like that. The girl was truly miserable. When I returned to the Pole I was as confused as ever. I came in and changed back into my civilian clothes, happy to find it wasn't quite six yet. I filed all my completed cases and started prep work for the next day. When it turned six I didn't waste a minute sticking around. I headed for the snowmobiles and waited for Justin.

A few of his sisters and cousins came out, hopping on their rides. Two even offered to give me a ride back but I waved them on, insisting I would wait for Justin. By six thirty I was cold and by seven I couldn't feel my toes anymore. Sighing deeply I headed back into the office. I passed through a series of halls and doors before I found my way to Justin's office. I started to knock but noticed the door was open. I slid inside to find an empty office. His coat was still here and his coffee was still warm. He hadn't gone far.

I stood leaning against his desk waiting for him to return. It was then I heard two voices arguing. One of them was Justin. "Just stay out of it. It's none of your business," Justin said firmly.

"I'm tired of seeing you get hurt. Let the girl go - she finished her cases, send her home. All that is going to happen is you'll get attached and when she leaves you'll be broken hearted again. It's been wonderful having you back, and I would really like to keep you." I then recognized the voice. It was Lucus. Even he thought I was going to break Justin's heart.

"From an operational standpoint it would be nuts to send her home. She finished her cases in less than a week. That never happens. You don't get rid of top performers this close to the show. As for my heart, let me worry about it." Justin's tone was deadly serious.

I wanted to rush in there, throw my arms around him and tell his father to give me a chance. I also knew that *that* was rushing it. I had an interview the next day that was for a job far away from here. Justin would never leave and I wasn't sure I could stay... or that I was even welcome.

Justin popped back in the office and was startled to find me. "Is it six already?" he asked, turning his wrist to look at his watch.

"Actually, it's past seven. I got cold waiting so I figured I would come in and see if I could give you a hand with anything." I did my best to appear unaware of his argument with Lucus.

"I'm really sorry. You should have just gone on without me." He seemed totally distracted. "Oh, hey, I heard you finished ten cases. That's really impressive. Do you think you'll be leaving soon?" he asked nonchalantly.

"I'm really enjoying my time here. My contract is until Christmas Eve, so I planned on staying here until then. I figured I could help with the backlog. There are a few cases that I think need extra attention and now I have the time to devote to them." I shrugged. "Unless you really want your room back."

"No, it's OK. You can stay as long as you like." He stopped. "You know what, I'm being selfish. You did your job. You should go home and see your family.

His words hit me like a slap. I just came to a crashing halt. I let out my breath slowly. "Are you really that worried about what people are saying? Or do you think your family is right and it's all just going to end in heartbreak?" I turned on my heel, ignoring his shocked face, and marched out of the office and then right out of the building. Thirty-five minutes later, frozen, angry, and fit to kill, I stormed into the little room we had come to share. I started to slam the door closed but couldn't bring myself to be that disrespectful.

Justin was already home, sitting in front of the fire. "You were already there. I could have given you a ride back."

I marched past him and went to the closet, throwing it open so I could pack. I tossed the suitcase open and just dumped my belongings into it. "Fine, you want me to leave, I'll go home." I forced myself to stop talking so I didn't say something I didn't really mean.

He came over and closed my suitcase. "Stop, you're pouting like a child. Haven't you heard the song - you'd better not pout because Santa Claus is coming to town."

"I have, but I'm pretty sure they only excluded assholes from the song because of the decade it was written in." I shoved the suitcase open.

He closed it again. "Don't leave. We could really use you and you're a lot of fun to be around."

"Look, Justin, I get it - you've been burned before. I may not have been around for centuries but the truth is I've been burned too. Yeah, this could end badly. It could end where we part as dear friends. Or this could be the best thing that ever happened to either of us, but if we let fear stop us before we even start then there is no point." I swallowed back what almost felt like a lump. "Be honest with me. I can handle the truth if you're not interested. Just don't jerk me around. You said you wanted to give this a shot, but if you don't want to anymore tell me."

He growled deep in his throat. "I want to give us a shot but I know you're going to leave. Everyone always leaves. My family has been guardians of this season for thousands of years. I have a bunch of sisters and even more cousins. Only Helen and I stayed. Everyone else left. If I can't count on my own bloodline, why would I be able to count on anyone else?"

"Wow, you really are broken aren't you?" I asked as I reached out to cup his cheek. "I can't promise we'll last forever, but I do promise one hell of a ride."

He turned his head and kissed my palm. "I'm more than seven times your age and you're better at this whole complicated emotional stuff than I am."

I smiled. "Yeah, I'm a product of the American public school system. If I didn't fall in love and want to crawl in a locker and die by lunch it was a slow day." He laughed. "If you want me to go home, I will. Give me permission and I'll go back and work from home. There is a lot of good I can do if you let me. If you want me to stay and we don't get any more involved, I can do that too."

"Grace, what scares me is that I already like you. I already worry about whether you are wearing enough layers and wonder what you did each day. My favorite parts of the day are the parts I spend with you. That's dangerous because like can turn into something more when you least expect it." He stood up and tugged me to follow him back to sit by the fire.

"Tell me what happened. Obviously, something happened," I urged.

His eyes shifted to someplace far off as he remembered. "It wasn't just one thing. It was a string of things. I've fallen in love and been dumped a dozen times. Last time was ten years ago. It was my sister's best friend. We had practically grown up together. She knew what it was like to be from up here. She came in over Thanksgiving weekend and we connected. The next three weeks were amazing. On Christmas Eve at the big Santa kickoff party I proposed. In front of everyone she said no then explained to me how she couldn't be stuck here. In private I offered to go with her. She told me that I would never be happy anywhere but here. She said staying with me would be like a cold, slow death sentence." He clapped his hands together. "So I swore off women."

"And did what? Date Polar Bears? I've been in bed with you. That was not nookie from an out of practice man. That was passionate and fun and really, really good." I almost sighed thinking about it.

He chuckled. "Glad to know you enjoyed it. I didn't mean I stopped being interested in woman. I just didn't get involved with them."

"Ah. I see." I was working my way through processing my feelings about the story when he hit me with the zinger.

"So what makes a girl who is obviously close to her family, and who talks to her Mom and Dad every day, move to the other side of the country and basically forget she's half Werewolf?"

I shifted uncomfortably and shrugged. "I finished school and got involved with a guy. We bought a house together and announced we were engaged. Then he disappeared and left me worried sick. When he reappeared he had found his Soul Mate and they had already been bound. So I was looking for a new job and I took the first one that would put an entire country between us. It's part of why I don't really like going home."

"Is he Were?" he asked

"Yep, part of Clan MacKay." I let out a heavy breath.

"Ouch, aren't your Clans deeply intermixed?" He actually winced as he asked.

"Yup, made better when his Soul Mate was my cousin Ella." I looked around the room for any reason to change the subject.

"Soul Mates are rare and really important in families like yours." He wrapped his arms around me, hugging me close.

"I know, and I don't hate them. It just makes family functions really awkward. Ella and I were really close. I don't have any sisters, but I had Ella." I leaned my head back against his shoulder.

"So what happens now?" he asked.

I was feeling as lost as he was. "I think we eat dinner." As if by magic, Joy knocked on the door, asking us if we were going to come eat.

Chapter Eleven

The week flew by. I returned to sleeping on the cot and it was like Justin was my best friend. We had tacitly agreed to enjoy each other's company but to otherwise cool our jets. I managed to clear out fourteen backlogged cases during the rest of the week, and by Friday, I was ready for the weekend.

I sat on the snowmobile waiting for Justin to finish work. One of his cousins appeared at my side. "Gracie, you guys are coming skating tonight, right?"

I blinked at her in incomprehension. "I have no clue. Justin hasn't mentioned it."

She smiled warmly. "Auntie Joy has been planning it all week. Even if Justin is grumpy, you should still come. It will be a lot of fun."

I thanked her and told her I would think about it. When Justin finally appeared something felt off. "Are you ok?" I asked as he slid on the snowmobile behind me.

"Huh?"

"Earth to Justin, come in Justin. Are you feeling alright? You look shook up." I looked at him over my shoulder but when he didn't answer I shrugged it off. Maybe it had just been a long week for him too. We dashed along the surface of the snow towards the main house. We arrived to be greeted by people heading out with their skates.

I bounced into the room looking for my skates. "Hey Justin, where did you put my skates?"

"Why?" He looked surprised.

"Because your mom has evidentially planned some big skating shindig on the lake and I want to get going." I looked under a pile of clothes in the closet.

"We don't have to go to that. We can stay in and relax if you want." I thought it was strange - he had obviously brought my skates from my house specifically for such a function and now he didn't want to go.

"I love skating. No matter how big the problems of the world seem, I always feel better when I'm gliding."

There was a knock on the door. "Come on in," I called over my shoulder, expecting Joy to pop in and ask if we were ready.

"Are you almost ready?" asked a chipper female voice I didn't recognize. I turned around expecting to see one of Justin's cousins or sisters. Instead there was a beautiful Halfling. She had small, pointed ears and the heart-shaped face of an Elf on a Dwarven body. She also had my skates hung over her shoulder.

She grabbed Justin's hand, giving it a playful tug. "I found these skates in the closet. They're really nice, I was surprised your sister gave them up."

I stood up. "She didn't. Those are mine." The girl's eyes turned and noticed me for the first time.

"Oh, I'm sorry. I didn't know. I thought they were Helen's old pair." She pulled them off her shoulder and held them out to me.

"No worries," I said accepting them. "I'm sorry, I'm Grace," I said, holding out my hand and smiling.

She took my hand, pumping it enthusiastically. "Hi, I'm Gwenna, Justin's fiancé."

A shocking pain clenched my head and heart. I slapped a hand over my eye as it began to twitch. I was sure I was having an aneurism. "I'm sorry, I wasn't aware that he had one."

She turned, poking him in the stomach. "I just accepted today."

I looked at Justin, who was pale. No wonder he was distracted on the way home. No wonder he had lost interest in me this week. I forced a smile to my face, still covering my twitching eye. "Congratulations."

Justin opened his mouth to say something but Gwenna cut him off. "We're going to tell everyone at the party tonight."

"Well then you'll need these." I handed her my skates. "I should stay in tonight and pack. I've finished all my cases so I think I'm going to head home early."

"Oh wow! That will be great for you. Most people don't finish this early. You must be really good at your job." Her smile was warm as she looped her arms around Justin's waist. We exchanged a few more pleasantries before they left.

I closed the door behind them, sinking to the floor. "What the hell just happened?" I asked nobody in particular. I spent the rest of the evening packing. I thought about taking down my decorations but I didn't want to think about the Holidays at all. He could just keep them, they were tainted.

I picked up my phone and dialed my mother. "Gracie? It's late, dear. Is everything ok?"

Somehow my Mom's all-knowing tone was all it took. I broke down, sobbing. "Justin just got engaged."

"Well that's exciting news! Joy and I knew there was something special between the two of you. We just didn't know it would happen so quickly." I pulled the phone away from my ear and looked at it as if that would reveal the trees obviously growing out my mother's ears.

"How do you know Joy?" I asked with a shaking voice.

"We're Facebook friends. We play those farming games together." I rolled my eyes. My mother had been obsessed with those games since she discovered them three years ago.

"Missing the point, Mom. He's engaged. I'm not." Just saying it caused all the air to leave my lungs.

"Well that doesn't sound right. Are you sure you heard correctly?" I wanted to cry harder. Where were the words of love and encouragement?

"Yes, Mom, I'm sure. I just met her." My throat hurt from the force of fighting back tears.

"Come home baby. Come back to your family who loves you. You've been gone too long. You'll come back, we'll have a nice holiday and you can heal." That was more like it. Only the idea of leaving hurt as much as staying.

"Mom, I don't want to go home. I think I just want to go back to Portland." I bit my lip. "I don't think I can handle Yule or Christmas this year. Tell people to just leave me alone. Please." She was silent on the other end of the line.

"I'll come out there. Your father and uncle can handle things here." I almost swore.

"No Mom, I'm a big girl. I'll be ok." I just wanted to crawl into a hole and lick my wounds.

"Gracie, you know we love you, right?" she asked finally.

"Yes, Mom. I know you love me." I took a deep breath.

"Don't do anything crazy. Alright?" It hit me then - between the job and this incident with Justin she was genuinely worried I would do something.

"Mom, I won't do anything crazy, I promise. If I think about it, I'll call." She seemed satisfied because she let me off the phone. I snuggled under the blankets on my cot and prayed sleep would come sooner than later. After another round of crying, sleep finally won out.

When I woke up the next morning the room was still dark. I could make out Gwenna's form on the bed, but she was alone. That at least made me feel mildly better. I quietly slid out the door and across the walkway into the kitchen. Joy was busy making breakfast. I tiptoed past her, hoping to make it to the bathroom undetected.

I brushed my teeth quickly. I wanted to just take care of my basic needs and go home. The fewer people I had to say goodbye to the better off I would be. I looked in the mirror finally and cringed. My hair was a wild tangle, my eyes were red and puffy from crying and my skin was pale. The black circles under my eyes almost marked me as undead. I looked away. Of course, she was beautiful and sweet - what wasn't to love? It must have been love at first sight.

When I re-entered the kitchen, Justin was talking to Joy. I thought I ducked fast enough, but they spotted me. Joy took one look at me and started to say something but I held up a hand. "I just want to go home," I said. Justin grabbed my arm and turned me around. I looked in his eyes and felt tears prick at my own.

"I'll take you. Are you ready to see your family?" I shook my head.

"I don't want to go to my parents' house. I just want to go home to my little apartment. I've had enough people the last few weeks. I don't think I could stand being at my parents' house." I pulled my arm free and walked back to the bedroom.

Gwenna watched from her spot on the bed as Justin helped me gather everything up. She didn't say a word as he tossed the fake snow into the air to take me home. The world shifted around us and soon we were standing in my dark little living room.

"Thanks," I mumbled as I took back my belongings he held.

"I'll bring you the decorations later this weekend. You'll need something to spruce this place up with." He forced a smile.

"Keep them, burn them, do whatever. I don't care, I don't want them anymore." I swallowed hard and closed my eyes. I knew if I looked at him I would cry.

"Grace, I know what this all looks like but it's not what you think." He started explaining it to me. "Gwenna was that girl I proposed to. I hadn't seen her since that night. She just showed up on Friday and said she was ready to settle down."

"I'm not mad. How can I be mad at you for being in love? I just wish I would stop getting attached to guys who can't give me their hearts." I opened my eyes to look at him. The tears started tumbling down my cheeks.

"I don't know what I want," he said. "She and I made so much sense. You and I feel like I always thought it would. I just don't know what to say or do."

"I think if the answer isn't obvious, I'm probably not that girl for you. I hope you're really happy."

He reached out and brushed away the tears. "Grace, I don't want to leave you like this. You don't deserve to be miserable like this."

"Yes, but you deserve to be happy." I forced a smile. "Go on and leave before this gets more embarrassing for me."

In a swirl he was gone. Somehow I found the strength to crawl to bed. I didn't leave it except to go to the bathroom and occasionally eat something. Hours passed, days passed and the only thing to mark the passing of time and alert the world that I was still alive was Netflix posting everything I watched on my laptop to my timeline.

When Yule came about a week later Mom called to check on me. She asked what my big plans were and I didn't have the energy to lie. "Watch Netflix, maybe order a pizza."

"Gracie, you've been home a week. All you've done is watch movies. You should go out, have fun. You're young and alive." I rolled my eyes.

"I don't feel good Mom. I just want to sleep."

"It's called depression, dear. If you can't snap yourself out of it then maybe you should talk to a doctor." I knew she was trying to be helpful.

"Am I crazy?" I asked.

"No, why would you say that? Depression doesn't make you crazy. It just means you're going through a rough time. Why do you think you're crazy?" She paused.

"I think I loved him the moment I met him. Like something inside me just turned on." I laughed. "That's the stupidest thing in the world though."

"No, it's not. When it's right, it's just right. I fell for your father the first day we met. I've loved him every day since. I know I told you that relationships are work, but some things - some things are just meant to be."

"I really do hope he is happy," I told her, the tears welling up inside me again.

"I know you do honey. I don't think you could hate someone if your life depended on it." Her words pushed me over the edge into rolling sobs again.

"Mom, I'm going to go back to bed. I love you." I hung up before she could make it worse.

I was just headed for bed when I heard a knock on the door. "Great. Now what? Have they come to evict me or something?" I mumbled to myself. I flung the door open with every ounce of anger I could muster.

"Hello, Grace." Lord Vallen's silky smooth voice greeted me. He took one look at me and asked, "Have I come at a bad time?"

I opened my mouth to say no but all that came out were sobs. He stepped in the doorway, closed his arms around me and let me cry. Occasionally he would stroke my hair, telling me it would all be alright. I don't know how long we stood there, but he didn't rush me or complain. He just stood there and let me cry, knowing it was what I needed most at that moment.

When I finally found my senses I wiped away the tears. "I'm sorry. I'm not normally so melodramatic. Why are you here? Is everything alright with the lantern?"

"Actually, Lady Jura's daughter Alizeyah stopped by with her friend the Pixie and her boyfriend the Werewolf. He was talking about the family gathering he was at and how happy they were for the diversion. We told them about the Holiday Spirit who helped us with the Lantern. It turned out that his cousin was a Holiday Spirit and couldn't be there at the gathering. We mentioned you were a Werewolf too, and lo and behold discovered you and Ian are cousins."

I blinked at him. He knew my cousin Ian because his girlfriend happened to be part of this Dragon household. What were the odds? "I see."

"Well, we mentioned that we had invited you to our gathering and he agreed it would be nice to see you. I called my friends working at the North Pole to find out what realm you were in and found out you left a week ago. I was very surprised to find that you were neither at our festivities, nor your family's, nor even the Dwarven Stronghold where it would seem you are a hero this season."

I shrugged. "I wasn't feeling the cheer."

"I can see that now." Lord Vallen paused for a moment, considering his words. "Do you know why we come together to celebrate Yule and the Bleak Days? Outside of the religious significance."

I shook my head. "Not really. Mainly just to see each other, I imagine."

"Well yes, that is part of it. Back before castles had fires that didn't die and Humans had electricity, we knew that winter would be hard. Every year it would claim some of our strongest. It didn't matter what race you were. Winter is cold and lonely, and if you let it, it will suck the life right from your lungs and leave you hollow inside. We would come together to give each other hope, warmth and strength. It also let us say goodbye, knowing some of those who we held wouldn't survive."

I thought about what he was saying. It made sense from everything I had read over the years. "So why are you here?"

"Because nobody should be alone to face winter when it arrives." He squeezed my shoulder. "You can get dressed and come with me to a gathering, or you can order some form of food this realm delivers. I've heard good things about both Pizza and Chinese. Either way, I won't let you face winter alone. That's what friends do." He offered me a half smile.

I went to my room and tugged on jeans and an oversized sweater. Vallen stood as I entered the living room again. He eyed me carefully, a frown creasing his brow, but he didn't say anything. I tugged on some boots and rummaged through the closet for my hat. "If it's your first pizza it should be the best in the area and unfortunately, they don't deliver. Do you mind a short walk?" I asked as I pulled the hat down over my ears.

"Not at all." Following me out the door, Lord Vallen took my hand and tucked it into the crook of his elbow. We walked along the quiet sidewalk, away from the rows of apartment buildings. Street lamps started to flicker to life as dusk approached. Clearing his throat he began to speak. "I have a friend that you remind me of. He recently met his Soul Mate, but he hasn't acted on their natural draw to each other."

I looked up at him. "Soul Mates are so rare, why would he not act on it?" I wasn't sure how this applied to me. Justin wasn't my Soul Mate - not in the magical meaning, at least.

"She is young compared to him and in love with someone else. He knows that because they are Soul Mates and have found each other that someday they will be together. For now he says he will wait. It's obvious to everyone but her that he is madly in love. I keep telling him all he needs to do is tell her the truth. Go to her and say, 'I love and I need you.'"

"Ah, I see where you are going with this. It's not that simple." I gave him a weak smile. "I barely know him and we're not Soul Mates. I have no claim to him."

"If love was simple, everyone would live Happily Ever After. Love doesn't play by a set of rules, it just exists. It happens slowly and it happens fast. Soul Mates aren't the only ones that have happy endings, or that have a strong love." I pulled us to a stop in front of a little hole-in-the-wall Italian restaurant. I opened the door and led the way in.

Lord Vallen looked around, taking in all the sights and smells. "What sort of meat and vegetables do you like?" I asked as I glanced over the menu.

He flashed a toothy smile. "Meat eats vegetables, therefore we can order extra meat and still get all our vegetables." I laughed, hard, for the first time in days. That was the sort of answer I expected from my brothers or my Wolfblood cousins.

"Ok, meat lovers it is." When the waitress came over I ordered us a couple beers and a meat-heavy pizza. She looked from Lord Vallen to me then gave me a way-to-go wink.

"Did that server just flirt with you?" he asked with confusion.

"No, she was signaling her approval of you." I smiled again.

"Human women are so odd," he responded, shaking his head. "I think you should tell Justin that you love him. If you don't, he could end up with the wrong person."

"Let's say I tell him how I feel and he rejects me. Then what? I've made things more awkward between us then they already are. He saw me crying - he knows I have feelings for him." I quieted as the waitress returned with our beers.

"I'm going to let you in on a little secret." Vallen leaned across the table and whispered. "Men... aren't always that bright when it comes to the affairs of our hearts." He leaned back in his chair and took a sip of the beer. His face turned almost green and he spit it back into the mug. "What is this swill?" he exclaimed in shock.

I couldn't stop it. Laughter bubbled over and erupted out of me. When I looked back at his face I just laughed harder. Everyone in the restaurant was now staring at us. When I was finally able to contain my laughter, I waved the waitress over and ordered him a soda. "That, my friend, is American beer."

"What a vile drink! Normally the Humans brew things almost as well as the Dwarves or the Dark Elves. That was horrendous. Never feed me that again. I'm sorry to sound like a rude guest, but seriously, that was horrible." I held up my hand as the waitress approached and sat a soda and with a straw in it in front of him. I held my breath as he took a sip.

His eyes lit up brightly and he smiled. "I don't taste a single drop of alcohol in that but it's delightful. What did you call it? Soda?" I nodded as he took another sip.

"I'm glad it's an improvement." I took another sip of my beer, resisting the urge to giggle when he cringed watching me.

"Anyway, as I was going to say before that disgusting decoction - you should still tell him. Even if he doesn't return your feelings you won't have anything to regret. You're half Werewolf. If you embrace your Darkling side, you'll have a very long life ahead of you. Wouldn't it be better to live without regrets?" I considered his words as the pizza arrived.

"Maybe you're right," I said, taking his plate and serving him up a large slice.

"Grace, I'm always right. It's the curse of being me," he said with an arrogant smile. He looked down at his slice of pizza, completely confounded on how to eat it.

I took the time to explain the intricacies of folding our pizza slices in half and eating them with our hands. Once shown the ropes Lord Vallen had soon consumed most of our pizza and asked if we might order a second. Laughing, I took pity on him and filled his Dragon belly with pizza and soda pop.

He walked me back to my apartment and thanked me for dinner. I pushed open the door to my place and looked around the bland little rooms. It felt naked. "Think it's too late to decorate?" I asked him.

He smiled. "No, you celebrate this realm's holiday called Christmas, right? That doesn't happen for a few more days."

"True. I'll have to see what I can come up with."

I watched as he rummaged through the pockets of his coat. "Lose something?"

He stopped and quirked a brow. "I am a Dragon. I don't lose things. I find them and keep them."

"Does that include ancient Dragon artifacts?" I teased.

He pulled a small pouch from his pocket. "I did not have charge of the artifact; if I had, it would not have been lost." He held the pouch out to me. "However, I am doing something that Dragons don't usually do. I am giving you a treasure. Consider it a thank you for your help. I think it may be of use to you."

I pulled on the strings of the pouch and opened it up. Inside was a black and silver bead, suspended on a chain. "It's beautiful, but I'm not sure how much I will use it. I don't really dress up much."

"It's a portal bead. I have one because I am a Dragon Lord, but I recently acquired this one from a Goblin who was less than honorable. Simply focus on it and tell it where you want to go. I figure you may need it to go talk to a certain someone. Just don't tell anyone where you got it. They're supposed to be registered with the OAC." He took it from me and helped fasten it behind my neck.

"Thank you, but why don't you give it to your friend who found his Soul Mate?" I played with the bead where it sat on my collarbone.

"Hue can already get from point A to point B without it. That and I'm not about to add to his treasure vault. He who dies with the most wins!" He chuckled. "I should get going. Thank you for dinner. I hope you will visit us next time."

"I guess I don't have a valid excuse not to. Thank you for coming. My head is clearer." I walked him out and watched as he disappeared in a ripple of wind. Stepping back inside, I looked around my lonely little apartment. He was right, I needed to give it a shot.

Chapter Twelve

I printed out a copy of my resume then packed my laptop, phone, charger, spare set of clothes and my ice skates. I tugged on my coat and boots, checked that I had my hat and gloves then tossed my bag over my shoulder. "Let's hope this goes well."

I closed my eyes and rubbed the bead on my necklace. I pictured the snow-covered North Pole and the warmth of the main house. I felt the air shift around me and a blast of cold swirl past. When I opened my eyes, there, fifty feet in front of me, was the main house. A feeling washed over me that filled me with warmth and courage.

I marched up to the house and pushed open the door to the kitchen. "Close the door, it's cold out there," Joy said, with her head shoved deep in the refrigerator. "If you're hungry there are leftovers in the fridge, otherwise Yule is in full swing. I'll bring out mugs of brew shortly." She sounded exasperated.

"I already ate, but I can give you a hand carrying the mugs." She jumped, smacking her head on a shelf within the industrial-sized ice box.

She whirled around wide-eyed and shocked. "Gracie, I didn't know you were here. Come in, dear. Sit down and get warm." She started fussing with the tea kettle.

"Joy, it's alright, I was only outside for five minutes." I smiled, setting down my bag. The Dwarven Mom rushed over, wrapping me in a bear hug.

"But what are you doing here, girl?" Her eyes sparkled warmly.

"I came to get what is mine," I smiled.

"I knew you would be back for your things. Justin said you told him to keep them. I know that when a woman is mad she says things she doesn't mean, though. I can gather them up for you." She started to turn around. Grabbing her arm, I urged her to have a seat.

"I'll take the brew out," I told her as I gathered up the mugs on a tray.

"Justin's out there. I don't want you or him to have to suffer any more than need be. Affairs of the heart are so painful," she said, patting my hand.

"I need to speak with Markus anyway," I told her, picking up the tray.

"Last minute Christmas Wish?" Joy grabbed another tray as a cheer went up from the great room. "I'll give you a hand." Joy followed me into the great room.

I began passing out mugs. When I got to the last mug I took a big sip and plopped down on Markus's lap. He was startled, but not as startled as Justin was, who was sitting next to him staring at me wide-eyed. "Santa, I know what I want for Christmas."

Markus smirked at me but rolled his eyes and played along. "Have you been a good girl this year?"

"Yes, very good. I was a top performer here and in my job back in the States," I told him.

"That's wonderful, Gracie. Tell Santa Claus what you would like." I reached into my back pocket and pulled out a folded paper, handing it to him. Markus reached around and opened it up to read. His eyebrows knit together in confusion. "Your resume? I don't understand."

"Santa, I want a job here at the North Pole." I put on an extra big cheesy smile like kids do for a picture or when they are trying to snowball the Mall Santas.

"You know, normally my HR or Ops people take care of this." He handed my resume to Justin.

"I realize that, but I wanted to know I got the job on my merits. If you hire me then there really isn't anything your Ops or HR people can do, right? After all, you are Santa." My smile brightened that extra watt.

"That is true. I am Santa, so really I am in charge. Consider it done." I leaned forward and hugged Markus.

"Thanks Santa!" Markus chuckled and helped me up. As soon as I was standing I smiled and plopped down on Justin's lap.

There was a surprised "Ooomph!" when I did. There were a few stifled chuckles around the room. "Justin Kringle, you are a huge pain in the ass." There was a gasp from everyone in the room. "You're a workaholic and a control freak that has to always be right."

I took his hand in mine. "You are also warm, unselfish, caring and thoughtful. I think I fell for you the moment we met. At the time I thought it was loathing, but now I'm pretty sure it was love. If you don't feel the same, that's ok. I just hope Gwenna is fine with seeing me all the time because I just took a job here."

He started to say something but closed his mouth. He took a deep breath and seemed to really study my eyes. Finally he spoke.

"Gwenna and I weren't engaged. She thought we were, but we weren't. I couldn't say anything at first because I didn't have a chance and then by the time we got in you were asleep and she had told the whole family. I was trying catch you before you left but it was a disaster."

His eyes were filled with hurt and anger. "You didn't hear me out, you just left. You leaving was horrible. I felt dead inside and now I'm just mad at you."

I hadn't considered this outcome. Everyone was staring at me and I felt severely out of place. I wanted to hop off his lap and go hide but I knew if I did that now it would just confirm his belief that I would run away again. "Well, you can just get over being mad at me. Forgiveness is a virtue. I spent an entire week crying over you. I only showered once. It took a

Dragon lecturing me to make me put on real clothes. If I can forgive you for all of that, including breaking my heart, surely you can forgive me for getting mad and scared and running away."

He slid me off his lap and I had to react quickly to keep from landing on the floor. "You left," he said, standing and leaving the great room. Dusting myself off, I squared my shoulders and walked back into the kitchen. Joy chased after me. "Gracie, don't leave. He just needs to calm down. Stay, at least for the night. I don't have a spare room, but the couch is pretty comfortable."

I turned and smiled at Joy. "Oh, I'm not leaving. I'm going to take my things, put them in our room and continue this conversation."

She blinked at me. "Do you think that's wise?"

"Yes. He obviously wants to punish me for leaving, but I think he needs a lesson in making people listen and communicating. I love your son. He may hate me now, but he is going to listen. He can still hate me tomorrow and that's ok because I am a professional and I love being a Holiday Spirit." She stared at me like I was crazy.

With a nod I picked my bag back up, and swung it over my shoulder. I grabbed my coat and gloves and marched out of the kitchen, across the walkway and to the door of our room. I tried to push it open and discovered it was locked. Cursing at him under my breath, I closed my eyes and focused on his room while touching the bead. The air shifted and grew warm.

I opened my eyes to the soft glow of the fire. The lights we hung still twinkled overhead. He hadn't taken anything down. "Why did you follow me?"

"Because you said you didn't have a chance to tell me anything, but I'm not going to let you run away like I did before I can say what I need to. I'm sorry I left and hurt you, but you went from being all passion to cold as ice overnight. Then suddenly a gorgeous Halfling shows up, claiming to be your fiancé, and you don't correct her. At the time I thought was getting out of your way. You didn't try to stop me from leaving either," I pointed out.

"I thought you wanted to leave and I wasn't going to make you stay against your will. It would be selfish of me to ask you to stay," he argued.

"Oh, like it would be selfish to stay and be in love with someone who has a fiancé?" I countered. "Let's be totally honest though. You've believed that I would run away from the beginning because that's what everyone does. Why would I be different? If you help push me out the door then it would be easier than watching me leave later? Right?"

Justin winced painfully at my words. "I came back because even if you didn't care about me, I wanted you to know I love you. I don't want to live the rest of my life asking if things would have been different." I leaned back against the hearth. "I came home just to tell you I wasn't leaving."

He got up out of the chair and wandered to the door. He fiddled with the locks for a moment then slid another one in place.

I stared at the row of locks on the door that were all new. "How many locks do you have?"

"One more than my mom has keys. Every time she figures out how to get in, I add another. I expect to need a new door by New Year's." I had to bite my lip to keep from laughing.

Pushing his sleeves up to his elbows and running his hands through his hair, he looked like a war was raging inside of him. Justin came to stand in front of me.

"You called this home." His eyes were hard and unreadable.

"They say home is where the heart is," I whispered.

"Then I'm glad mine is back where it belongs." He slid his arm around my waist, then tugged my head back with my ponytail. Before I could ask what he meant, he captured my mouth with his. It was a demanding and possessive kiss, the kind you expect when a lover comes home from war. One that says, you're back and I'm never letting you leave again. I melted against him, wrapping my arms around his neck and refusing to let go. When finally we broke the kiss gasping for air, he swept me up into his arms and carried me to the bed. We all but fell into the pile of blankets. It was a wild torrent of arms, legs and lips as we did our best to strip each other out of our clothes.

Justin sat on the bed, resting his hands on my hips. His gaze seemed to caress every curve of me. When he tugged me forward, he hugged me close, pressing his ear to my chest, listening to my heartbeat. With slow, deliberate moves he began kissing a path down my breast until he reached its already hardened tip, which he sucked greedily into his mouth. My head fell back and I moaned.

He held me close with one arm while he playfully caressed my inner thigh with his fingertips. He urged me to open my legs wider for him. Carefully he stroked the soft lips of my sex. Teasing it until I ached with need. He slid his fingers within me, causing my knees to buckle. He steadied me on my legs, but slid his between my knees, forcing me to open wider and expose myself more to his touch. Justin held me in place, unable to sit or kneel as he continued to stroke me.

I begged him to let me feel him inside me but he continued to caress me intimately until I couldn't take it any longer. An overwhelming release rushed through me, causing me to scream and rub myself against the hand that still continued to massage me. My knees buckled again and I threw my arms around his neck to keep from toppling over onto him. His caress made me feel like my entire womanhood was on fire and burning hotter and hotter. Another wave of pleasure ripped through me as I rode his hand between my legs.

This time when my legs turned to jelly beneath me he tugged me forward so that I would straddle his hips. He guided me effortlessly down onto his shaft where I moaned at the pure pleasure of him being deep inside me. He took a shaky breath. "You feel ... if there is a heaven when I die and it doesn't feel half as good as this, I'm coming back to wander the Earth with you." My laugh was cut short when he flexed his hips and pressed deeper into me.

Using my hips as a guide he urged me to move in slow thrusts that took him deeper into me. Each one caused him to take a shuddering breath. He steadily tried to build speed, but I was enjoying him slowly losing his composure. In a total act of defiance he cupped my derriere, stood up without withdrawing, turned to face the bed and then buried himself hard and deep into me as he lowered us back onto the mattress. I started to protest but he leaned down, biting my lip playfully, and drove himself quickly into me again. He kept the intensity hard and deep, but hands on my hips he drove me to a frenzy with his speed. The only word I could remember was his name, which I kept gasping until my entire body spasmed around him. Tiny fireworks exploded behind my eyes, matching the pulses running through my body. He cried out his own release as one last thrust buried him so deep it felt like he reached my heart.

There, as we lay combined as one, panting for air, he leaned his head against mine. "I love you Grace MacGregor. You're never allowed to leave without me again because I don't think I can live without my heart."

I smiled and snuggled close to him as he dragged the covers over our shaking bodies. "I don't think I'll ever get tired of making love to you."

"That's good, because I plan on doing it for several more centuries." He chuckled before falling asleep.

I pondered his words carefully. Obviously I was forgiven, but did he really mean what he said about several more centuries? The thought of not having him with me made me hope that his words weren't empty phrases made in vain during an erotic moment of bedsport.

"I want that too," I whispered as I ran my hand along his cheek. He kissed my fingertips and mumbled some lovely words. When I finally fell asleep I dreamed of the type of life we would have together.

I decided the next morning that I liked the locks on the door. It made it almost impossible for someone to barge in. I unpacked the few belongings I had brought, showered, and rode into the office with Justin. After all, as a full-time employee, there was paperwork to fill out.

When I stepped back into the office all the Spirits stopped and stared at me. "Oh, don't worry. I don't officially start as manager of Holiday Spirit and Good Will until the New Year. I just have two or three cases I want to take care of." I sank into the chair at my desk and flipped the computer on.

I sifted through Facebook until I found Frank Martin. For nearly ten years Frank had been trying to find his birth mother who had given him up forty years ago because she was a single mother who had lost her husband in a fatal accident. I sent him a message with a link to the cranky old cat lady. I made it a point not to tell him that's how I thought of her.

To finish up the case, I contacted the company in New York. They had offered me a job as an executive assistant last week. I thanked them for the consideration, but let them know I had found something that was the perfect fit and walking distance from home. I also played with a little magic snow and convinced them I had the perfect candidate for the job. I hung up the phone and signed off that both cases were done.

"I'm going out," I said, tugging the white wool duster on and pulling the hood up. The office stared at me as I twinkled off to do my good deed. When the world settled back to normal around me I climbed the stairs of the old Victorian house and rang the doorbell. As expected, the Cat Lady's assistant answered the door.

She looked at me all clothed in white and raised a brow. "Hello, can I help you?" she asked.

"Hi there Rosa, you don't know me but I'm your very own Holiday Spirit, sent by the North Pole." I dug around in my pocket and pulled out the stack of papers which had been my employment contract for the New York job. I handed her that and my ticket voucher. "Santa has seen what a good girl you've been this year. He says you should go be closer to your family and be with them through the Holidays and beyond. Here is a ticket and a job waiting for you there," I smiled.

She stepped outside onto the steps and looked around. "Where are the cameras?"

I blinked. "What cameras?"

"The ones where you jump out and tell me this is a joke." She leaned further out to look down the street.

"All totally legit. You can call the number on the contract and voucher to make arrangements and see that it is all taken care of." I nodded at her. She looked at the paper in her hands.

"What about Ms. Dally? She can't be left alone." I smiled at her as she looked at me skeptically, waiting for the catch.

"I've taken care of everything. I swear."

Without warning she launched herself at me in a hug. "Thank you. I can't explain it, but I believe you. Everything's going to be alright."

I shrugged. "It's what I do. Merry Christmas, Rosa." I turned and walked away, letting a swirl of snow take me home.

When I got back Justin was sitting on the edge of my desk in the office. I looked around and everyone was gone. "Was I gone that long?"

"No, I just sent everyone home early. I figured you closing two cases without even being on the clock was as good as any reason. Everyone is done with their cases anyway." I stepped forward into his open arms.

"Actually, I closed three today." I kissed him on his cheek.

"The crazy cat lady and assistant are technically one case. Then there was the guy looking for his mom. What other cases?" I reached behind him and pulled out a file that had a coffee ring on it.

"Ten years ago a very sweet but stubborn man had his heart broken tragically on Christmas Eve. The Holiday Spirits have been trying to heal it since then, but none have succeeded." I smiled, pressing a kiss to his lips, pulling his ponytail free of its tie so I could play with his hair. It tumbled and twirled wildly around my fingers.

He pulled free of my grasp to open the file. I did my best to distract him. I even went for his ears. Elves, Dwarves and Fae all have such sensitive ears. He gasped and melted at my touch just a little but won the war pulling free. "I can't believe they had a file on me." I snagged it out of his hands. "Hey, I was looking at that."

"Are you satisfied with the service you received?" I teased.

"Yes ma'am, I will make sure to write your manager a letter and let him know about the excellent service I received." He kissed me again.

"Is there anything else I can help you with today?" A grin pulled at my lips.

"Actually, yes." He let go of me long enough to pull a small red box from his pocket and open it. Within was it was a ring in the shape of a snowflake. He sank to one knee in front of me and looked up with a mixture of fear and hope. "Marry me and make every day of my life a holiday worth celebrating."

"That was really corny," I said pinning him with my gaze. "I happen to like corny. I'll add that to the list of things I love about you."

He slid the ring on my finger, staring at it there for a moment. When he stood it was to claim my mouth in a kiss that promised many years and a lifetime of happiness.

"Does this mean you'll be my date for New Year's?" I asked.

"Yes, and just wait until you see New Year's North Pole style."

I shook my head and grinned. "No, wait till you see it with an entire house filled with Scottish and American Werewolves."

His eyes narrowed on me. He considered me for a moment then finally nodded. "Sorry, I had to consider if I loved you enough to risk being mauled as your new fiancé."

"And?"

"I would risk Werewolves for you. I would even leave the Pole for you. I can't imagine loving anyone more than I love you."

ABOUT THE AUTHOR

Isabelle Saint-Michael is a cupcake enthusiast, shoe addict, and world traveler. She is known for her sense of adventure and geekier hobbies. She is frequently seen haunting coffee shops and pubs in the wee hours of the morning. No matter where she goes, shenanigans and laughter are never far behind.